Classified Hearts

Aimee Blanc

This is for those of us who deal with RSD (rejection sensitivity dysphoria) and imposters syndrome.

You are enough as you are.

And know you're not alone ❤

(I'll note that this isn't something the characters deal with, but I personally battle with regularly).

ISBN -13: 978-0-473-72506-8

Contents

Authors note

This author is a New Zealander; therefore, it is written in Australian English (please don't ask me how this makes sense). I have made all the efforts to get rid of any 'Kiwi' slang, and there is an explainer for the Russian words at the end, including the meaning of some of the names as I think it adds to the story.

Also, I'm writing this in a fictional world where Russia respected Ukraine's borders (dating back to Crimea) and never started a war. I do not, and never will condone war. ✌

I hope you love Misha and Matt as much as I do. Also, let me know if you need to know Sasha's story... Because that's simmering away in the background. However, Babushka's is coming first.

Triggers: this book covers a few darker themes, including racism, alcoholism, kidnapping and torture. There is mention of violent deaths, but they are historic.

For a full list of triggers feel free to contact me.

Mum and Gran, if you're reading this, do me a massive favour and skip chapter 27. That way I can still look you both in the eyes over Christmas dinner. ❤

Chapter One - Misha

It's one of the biggest nights of the year for people like me. If not the biggest night in the four-year election cycle. Individuals like me who live off the energy in the air. The thrill, the sense that change is just around the corner and that you, you as an individual, had something to do with it. That you were an integral part of helping people, or advocating for people who had all but given up on the political system.

The poll booths are minutes away from closing and there's an electric buzz in my campaign office.

The office isn't far from my apartment—just a short walk around the corner. It's based upstairs in the main shopping centre in the suburb. The salty breeze plays through my hair as I stand outside it, admiring the effort it has taken to get to this point.

The fluorescent lights overhead cast a bright glow on the bustling office. The walls of the campaign headquarters are covered in posters, each one brightly coloured and adorned with slogans and promises. People in suits rush around with clipboards and phones, their faces filled with determination and hope.

The clock on the wall ticks closer and closer to closing time.

The sound of hushed conversations and excited voices fills the room, creating a hum of energy and anticipation. The air is filled with the sweet taste of champagne. An atmosphere of anxious excitement lingers, heightening the senses of everyone in the room. I can feel my stomach flipping with nerves, the fear of letting down all my supporters, those who voted for me, by not winning leaving a bitter taste in my mouth.

I ran for a role as a member in the New South Wales parliament this year, my first foray into politics. A friend convinced me to run one day when I was complaining about how much positive change I could make. If only I had a little bit of sway and power to do so in the community. I could not only stand for people who immigrated, but also have the chance to keep those who have been known to exploit poorer communities held to account.

The votes are rolling in, and while it doesn't feel like it's the highest of stakes, it's only state government after all, it still feels important. It feels important to me. It feels big to that little girl who moved to Sydney from Russia. Whose family scrimped and saved for years after the fall of the Soviet Union to move away from Russia so that their children might have a better future. It's been instilled into me from my upbringing to give back to the country that welcomed a bedraggled and wide-eyed family of Russian immigrants over twenty years ago. I want to give back to Australia and help others in my position to find safety and solace here.

I ran independent of any political party. I felt like political affiliation would possibly be a hindrance for someone like me. Someone perceived to be different.

An immigrant.

An outsider.

I was teased mercilessly as a child for my accent, especially when we first came over. They joked I must be related to the leaders in the Kremlin, that my family and native country were the epitome of evil. It wasn't hard to tell where these kids' views and opinions had come from. The Cold War didn't directly involve Australia, but the country is closely aligned with the United States of America. Australia is also a country whose people can be a bit closed-minded with anyone they don't agree with. That's why I'm running. Sure, it might open me up to much more harm, like death threats, sexual assault threats or harassment. But it means another little girl who is also fleeing her home country can see someone like me becoming a member of the New South Wales parliament, and know it's possible for them too. What's to stop the likes of a Syrian refugee from becoming a member of the federal parliament of Australia?

My thoughts are broken by a loud countdown from my colleagues,

"FIVE!

FOUR!

THREE!

TWO!

ONE!

Voting has closed!

"Let's all raise a glass to our work and of course our candidate, Mikhaila Zaitseva!"

We all raise a glass in toast to the work we had done over the last several months, and for some, over the last several years.

"All right team! Gather round," I called out, tapping on my champagne glass and trying to get the excited crowd's attention. I was preparing to give a rousing speech about how it doesn't matter what happens in that final vote count, and that I am proud of them all. Someone turns the volume up on the television and I'm ignored, as the state broadcaster starts showing numbers coming in.

I watched in disbelief as the numbers that were updated on the large TV at the end of the room start to gather momentum...

In my favour!

Picking my jaw up from the floor, as people jostle around me, I yell "GUYS!" at the top of my lungs which this time caught their attention.

"I just wanted to thank everyone for the tireless work we've all put in over the last few months. I know it looks promising right

3

now," I pause to allow a loud cheer to die down, " but as my Babushka used to say; your elbow is close, yet you can't bite it."

I faced the crowd, most of whom had confused looks on their faces. Russian proverbs can do that to people.

"It means, while we're close to the win, we don't want to celebrate until it's official. I don't want to celebrate too early, but know that I am so damn proud of the effort each and every one of you has made, so from the deepest part of my heart, thank you."

The night continued with the typical election night fanfare, loud gasps when the numbers became close in the ticking up of counted votes, drinks flowing freely, as were most people's opinions of both me and the incumbent member for Vaucluse.

I was used to it, the thinly veiled Russophobia bordering on discrimination, despite the effort I've put in for my community, and how I worked hard for all Australians. The people in attendance tonight are part of the effort to get me elected, so it wasn't hard to ignore any negativity about my birth country, especially as the gap between me and my competitor, a man who has been an outright Russophobe and is often racist towards other marginalised communities, widens and I take a strong lead.

I feel a guilty sense of glee as the vote count closed for the night. Not only had I provisionally won, but I expelled someone who harmed the greater community instead of advocating for it. He advocated for his own back pocket and the back pocket of other wealthy members of the district. Cheers are erupting around the room, and I feel so fortunate that all these people's hard work wasn't for nothing.

I kicked off my heels, head buzzing still from the win, and groaned at the feeling of gaining sensation back into my toes. Sighing as I entered my empty apartment. I wished that on nights like these, when I've got something to celebrate, that I had someone to come home to and celebrate with.

Of course, my family is overjoyed. I called them during my car ride home. I heard my Mama crying, and Papa's gruff exterior cracking with pride in his tone, warming my heart. My brother, as usual, was unreachable due to the hours he holds running his restaurant, but there was only one other person I wanted to call.

I dialled the international number, hoping I wasn't interrupting one of her infamous teatime sessions with the other Babushkas in the surrounding apartments. She's been known to invite the other widowers around to gossip, play cards, and drink tea. It was her way of finding out what was happening in her neighbourhood.

"Zaychik! It is very good to hear from you," my grandmother says as the call connects. Her thick Russian accent fills the line and her broken English from lack of practice always fills my heart, she tries harder when she knows those of us who moved to the West will be tired.

"Babushka, I did it," I say in an outburst, unable to hold my excitement but equally hoping she hasn't forgotten what I was doing today, well yesterday now. It was two am in Sydney, but six pm over in the part of Russia she lives in.

"Bozhe moi, Zaychik! We must celebrate" she declares, "You won, no? And got that old white man who hurt my Zaychik's feelings out of power?"

I cringe at how she's put it, but my grandmother has been known to be blunt. Can't expect her to change after all this time.

"Da, Babushka, he's not in office anymore. I'm the representative for Vaucluse which includes Bondi and the community Mama and Papa live in."

We continued the conversation for a little while longer catching up on the latest news from her friends, and her catching up with news from my family, until I found myself yawning.

"Oh Zaychik, I forget myself. It must be incredibly late for you to be calling, please go. Please get some rest. But also book flights to come and visit your Babushka soon, no? I miss your face."

I grumbled at that, explaining to her that she wouldn't miss it as much if she allowed her family to set her up with Skype or Zoom, but no. She is very traditional and must have a landline connection in case anyone her age needs to get in touch with her. The fuss with those video calls was beyond her.

"Da Babushka, I will book flights soon, and I will go now and rest. Have a lovely evening."

The conversation closed with the usual good nights, and I turned to face out towards the windows of my apartment, watching people walk past on the street below, coming home from a night out.

The view from my two-bedroom apartment wasn't much but having my own space gave me a sense of freedom I haven't ever had, even while studying. I got to experience it after I graduated. I turned from the window, closed the curtains, and walked to the kitchen counter to put my phone on charge before heading to bed.

I know tomorrow will be the start of a new chapter and I drift off to sleep satisfied with the idea that what I was doing was for the right reasons.

Chapter Two - Misha

The next couple of months that followed that night went by in a whirlwind.

I've finally been formally sworn in, but then had to prepare for the job by reading screeds and screeds of reports and documents. My head is still swimming with data about the state, and the different districts. The different portfolios the state legislative branch covers, and I couldn't be happier. I felt like I might finally be able to make some changes.

Walking into my office, I collapsed on my chair and flicked my computer mouse to get my day started again. It's the third week in office and portfolios are about to be divided out among us. I was just getting used to standing for the people of Vaucluse, with meetings and office hours set up in my district, and I was setting up further appointments with constituents when Sasha called.

"Privet, Misha speaking," I say as I pick up the call. Only greeting Sasha in Russian as I know it's her. She and my Babushka are the only ones I greet that way anymore.

"Privet Misha!" My best friend Sasha greets me brightly,

"Are you free for lunch today?"

Lunch was always our way to catch up especially since Sasha went from her master's to PhD study, then topped it off with working near full-time hours with the Russian consulate here in Sydney. Her only free time these days was her lunch break, she usually tended to work late at the consulate, matching the time zone the Muscovites worked in. Halfway between the university and getting to work was one of our favourite stops, and I got off the tram there, waiting outside in the warm Sydney sunshine for my friend.

Ordering lunch, we caught each other up on our goings-on and got talking about what the first few weeks on the job were like for me, the good and the bad.

"It's all a bit overwhelming if I'm honest," I explain to Sasha.

She sips her coffee and murmurs in agreement.

"I had no idea just how much reading and conversations and…" I trail off, thinking about how fast some of the people tasked with helping us talk and remembering that, while I'm fairly quick when speaking English, I still translate a lot of speech from English into Russian in my head before I respond in English. It's exhausting and I feel overwhelmed even just thinking about it.

"Gah, it's all just a lot." I sigh, then realise how it might have come across, "Not that I'm ungrateful or anything! I'm so thankful to have been elected and be representing my community. I just mean that because I didn't have any political knowledge going into this, I'm just a tad overwhelmed and highly underprepared." I finish with a nervous chuckle.

Sasha stared at me then, "Are you in over your head Misha? Do you need help?"

Her stare cuts through me, those blue eyes filled with concern and knowing how I act when I'm overwhelmed.

I shook my head vehemently, knowing exactly where this was going.

"No, no, no, no. I have help."

"Would it help if I came upstairs and helped tidy perhaps? I know when you're highly stressed how untidy things around you can get." She says to me with her left eyebrow cocked. She sees right through me; she has since we first moved in across from each other at Wesley College.

Sighing again, I picked up the tab for lunch and I made my way back towards the office in the New South Wales Parliamentary buildings.

I glance behind me and see Sasha buried in her phone, no doubt looking at a hot match on one of her dating apps or dealing with an email about her PhD, judging by the intense way she's looking down at her phone. I wait for a few more seconds to see if she notices my disappearance.

"Are you are coming?" I call over my shoulder to Sasha. Her brow gathers as she finishes furiously typing on her screen then looks up to see me at the door and quickly gathers her purse. She rushes up to me, so we can exit together, and I can get her signed in with security at the parliamentary buildings.

Up in my office, I have to admit that Sasha was correct. There were briefings and speech drafts strewn everywhere, and I knew I needed to tidy it all up and get the space sorted just in case someone from my district showed up out of the blue.

"Hey," I say towards Sasha, who is walking into the room wide-eyed, with a touch of fear marring her beautiful face. This woman knows me well. Possibly a little too well.

"There's possibly some confidential stuff in here. Can we please keep anything that you might see in here between us?"

She nods and tentatively starts on the closest pile of papers, simply picking them up, making sure they're all up the same way, portrait, and placing them in a tidy pile on my desk.

This isn't the first time Sasha has helped me out when I'm overwhelmed. When we lived together, while we were studying, she was always one of the first people to pick up when I had a particularly stressful presentation to give, or a short assignment lead time coming up. She always took on the job of tidying up, and in return, I always made sure she had good food when she came home from work or university. Perks of growing up with a chef in training.

A feeling of lateness came back to me in that moment. A memory of being late on one of my master's assignments. And when I say late, I mean I felt like I was running behind, but realistically I was writing and researching weeks before other students had started. I always had a few issues with anxiety and timelines. Sitting in my room, headphones on with a mixture of George Ezra and Ed Sheeran blasting while I read up on the latest news from America in the run-up to their presential election. It was honestly like watching a soap opera in slow motion and was study adjacent. I hear a timid knock on my bathroom door and get up and go over to see who is there. Most normal people tend to knock on the front door, but Sasha and I moved in together for post-grad to save money and have always had a bathroom between our rooms.

I was too slow to get up from my bed, surrounded by open textbooks and a table nearby with a variety of drinks, notably a half-drunk iced coffee and an empty can of energy drink. And there was Sasha, in the bathroom doorway, grinning, but shaking her head at my messy nature. I had a bad habit of holing up in my room and procrastinating or hyper-focusing on study.

Sasha, a PhD student at the University of Sydney, was one of the first people I met in undergrad. When the people who sorted out halls of residents obviously thought putting the two Russian girls in rooms next to each other and sharing a bathroom, would be a hoot.

But my upbringing couldn't be more different from Sasha's. My family struggled in Russia, and still do if I'm being honest with myself. Babushka is the only one still there.

Sasha's family did well out of the fall of the Soviet Union and set themselves up comfortably in St Petersburg. I'm not jealous, she didn't have it completely easy, as her parents' love was missing from her upbringing. She came to Sydney for a fresh start. A way to get away from her family. She is determined to stay if she can, with the condition of her stay in Australia being only for as long as she's studying imposed by her father.

"Where does this go?" She lifts up a flash drive found near an empty coffee takeaway cup over the other side of the room, jerking me out of my daydream about our shared past.

"Oh! Um. I'm not sure who might have left that here. I'll get IT to have a look at it to make sure it's safe, then have a look." I say trying to think about who might have left it behind. Who had visited recently that may have mentioned a flash drive I needed to look at later? I'd been meeting with other politicians and policymakers, students, and people from my district, and in that whirlwind, it could be anyone.

Sasha shrugged and popped it down on top of the pile of papers on my desk.

The tidy-up was successful, and probably for the first time since this became my office, it felt tidy and like mine.

"Thank you so much, Sasha! I have to run to a meeting with some of the other members, but could we pretty please catch up for dinner soon?"

She nods with a smile and goes to pick up her purse.

I run over to her, and crash tackle her small body with a bear hug, "What would I do without you?"

"Nothing good I'm sure," she winks as she leaves the office space, and my phone dings with my next meeting and a new email.

Not with the meeting I was expecting nor an email anyone wants.

To: Mikhaila Zaitseva

From: Robert Peterson

Subject: !! URGENT MEETING REQUEST!!

Misha, this meeting is urgent.

Something has occurred in New Zealand's parliament that closely relates to you and your position within this state's legislative branch. Can you please come to my office as soon as possible?

Robert Peterson

Speaker of the Legislative Assembly of New South Wales

Shit.

I grabbed my laptop and swept the pile of documents and all other content on my desk into the top drawer, slamming it closed.

Slamming the door shut as I fast-walked down the hall to Peterson's office, I worried about what I might have done wrong already in my first few days. My mind raced with all the appointments I'd had, and if I somehow put my foot in it during that time. Or if someone accused me of doing something because of my heritage.

Though he did say it had something to do with the New Zealand parliament. And while they are close to us Australians, due to our countries' different sizes our political systems are quite different. What could have happened to get me pulled into my boss's office, especially something that occurred over the other side of the Tasman Sea?

Chapter Three - Misha

The midday news was playing on the television in his office, the TV screen set to a news network from New Zealand.

It's never a good sign to see this coming into your boss's office. It signalled the beginning of a scandal.

I tentatively knocked on the door frame, not wanting to disrupt any conversations that might be occurring but also knowing that Robert was expecting me, I could hear the presenter talking.

It can be revealed as an exclusive to this news network that list MP, Ismail Aliev has been escorted off the premises at the Beehive in Wellington this morning. He was escorted by police and has been remanded in custody. This is after the explosive accusations of espionage that occurred late last night in an urgent sitting of parliament. For more on this, we cross live to our reporter Lily-Jean, who is outside Parliament.

Lily-Jean, is there more you can tell us?

The TV volume was lowered quickly, and Robert yelled, "Come in!"

I gulped as I walked in, feeling guilty somehow.

"Have you seen this?" Robert points at the screen as it crosses back to the man presenting the midday news.

The presenter was further explaining how there's been a major security breach in New Zealand's parliament creating a major political scandal for the country. That and it's connected to the Russian government.

"No sir," I reply timidly.

I was used to a bit of Russophobia but seeing my home country commit these kinds of espionage crimes gave some of the behaviour I had previously experienced some reason.

"So what am I to make of this? A Russian man was elected in New Zealand just last year, and he has now leaked confidential information about military alliances, government weaknesses, and pointers on how to exploit New Zealand's international footing straight to the Kremlin and now we've just elected a Russian woman." He stares at me pointedly. The stare cuts to my core, even though all of his accusations are completely unfounded.

I know what he was getting at, despite this I wasn't used to quite so much bigotry from him, which caused me to pause before choosing whether or not to speak.

I gulp knowing there's unlikely to be much I can say right now, while this whole thing is imploding over the Tasman, that Robert will actually believe. Much less the risk-averse New South Wales Premier.

"With all due respect sir," I start, though he scoffs at me.

"Just because I was born in Russia, doesn't make me a spy. New South Wales did a full background check on me and my family. There are no links back to the Kremlin, the KGB, or the FSB. My family left Russia 25 years ago. When we lived in Russia, we were a poor fishing family that lived on the other side of the country from those in power. On the East coast of the largest country on the planet, in Asia, not Europe."

He rolls his eyes at me, "Yeah and our mates across the Tasman are now in hot water because they trusted a bloke who claimed he was from Dagestan. The New Zealand parliament and the political parties trusted him at his word. And now they find out that his father is an active FSB agent. How am I to trust where your allegiances lie?"

Each word slashes across my skin like a knife. I've lived in Australia for 25 years and I'm still treated like an outsider. A villain, all because of the happenstance of my birthplace.

I'd been elected by Australian citizens to represent them, at the state level, but that wasn't anything to scoff at. Still, the circumstances of my birth, being born in Moscow when the Soviet Union was still in existence, with spying and espionage running rife, and now a kleptocracy in power over there still haunts me.

It follows me everywhere I seem to go.

I let Robert's words sit with me for a second before a cold rage settles across my skin causing me to shudder. I straighten my shoulders, sit up straighter, and prepare for the oncoming verbal spat.

"Sir," I ground out through my clenched teeth, "What do you want me to do? Renounce my citizenship to my birth country? Do you want to wiretap my office? My phone? My home? Have someone follow me around 24/7 like a prison guard in my country, in my own home? Do you want to read all my correspondence home?

My parents live in Bondi, Robert. And yes, my grandmother lives in Moscow, but she's the only family still back in Russia. Do you want to read all my correspondence to her? Do you want me to translate that all for you too? Because it's all in Cyrillic and I know there are very few who can read that around here. Also, Dagestan is a part of modern-day Russia as well. Something you ought to know." I finished glaring at him.

"Sit down Mikhaila." He spits sharply.

I keep glaring at him and stay standing.

"Fine." He says as he does something on his phone and the TV screen to my right flickers, the one that was showing the news only minutes ago.

Hello.

The TV starts, the Prime Minister's voice coming out of the speakers, before the picture connects and it's him sitting in his office staring down the barrel of the camera. It has an eerie effect of making me feel like he's watching me, that he himself thinks I'm guilty of what Robert has all but said out loud.

You've been called into your superior's office because of a major threat of espionage at all levels of the Australian government. And before you blame this on the New Zealand case, we've had word from the Kiwis that this isn't contained in their borders. It's suspected that most major Western governments may have also been subjugated to this same network of illegal information sharing. This is highly classified information. Sharing it outside of this room is considered an act of treason. We are looking at all our people in Government as part of a risk profile done by the Australian Secret Intelligence Service. You have been deemed a high risk. This could be due to a few factors, but we will try to clear your name, should your name be able to be cleared. Your superior will update me, and the ASIS may also contact you. Once we have more information on the national security threat and situation, you will have further information on your fate.

"I will follow up on this with my boss and the Premier. I suspect some form of surveillance will be done. This isn't a personal slight on you. This isn't a Russophobia thing," I snorted at this feeble attempt at trying to mask his own prejudices and at calming me down while he turned the TV off.

"However," he continues to ignore my attitude towards the situation, "we need to tread carefully. We don't know if we've also been infiltrated in the New South Wales parliament or federal parliament. Every single level of government, every state in the country, is doing this kind of thing Mikhaila. We need to be careful. We need you to prove you're not a spy. " He stated carefully.

I rolled my eyes at that. Careful. Sure. As an excuse for racism or anti-immigration stances, this takes the cake. A chance that ideas like these, considered abrasive in polite company can now be spoken aloud because of a 'political emergency'. Also, me, a spy?

The last time I tried to do anything remotely sneaky I was brought to my knees with guilt thinking about how my Babushka would handle me or any kind of deception.

I bought my chin up and said "I have nothing to hide. Other than my grandmother and childhood house, I have no ties to Russia and no ties to the Russian government. I've never even paid tax there. I'd be happy to renounce my citizenship to my birth country if I must have someone follow me, I'm happy to do almost anything. I just want to serve my community and do the job they elected me to do".

"Okay Miss Zaitseva, we will be in touch about what we're going to do about this situation. You need to clear your calendar for the next few months or so and cancel any appointments with constituents while we get this all cleared up. Or at least have your office take care of any important appointments." He said formally.

"We will get this cleared up, and I'm sure, get your name cleared."

I huff at that, of course, my name will be cleared, I'm innocent of what he's accusing me of.

I guess it was a good thing the premier was slow to assign portfolios because clearing my calendar of all of that work would have been painful. For me and anyone else who is going to help me sort out my office during this mess.

"But know this Mikhaila Zaitseva, if you're found guilty, of sharing information with foreign governments in any way shape, or form, you will feel the full force of the Australian federal government. You won't be an Australian anymore, and you won't ever get to see your family here. I don't care how popular you are in Bondi, or how respected your brother is. I will personally put you on the next flight leaving Sydney bound for Moscow."

I blanched at the idea of losing my family and leaving them behind in Australia. At how that might break my family after we had worked so hard to assimilate into Australian culture and become part of the Russian expat community here.

Robert dismissed me by dialling a number on his phone and turning his office chair away from me and towards the window facing the street.

"G'day mate!" He starts his call and I take that as my cue to leave. To pack up the office I had worked so hard for and find a half-decent vodka to take with me to visit my brother at his restaurant.

Chapter Four - Matt

My day started like any other. Traffic through Sydney's M1 this morning was bumper to bumper, causing me to be late. My coffee was, of course, lukewarm by the time I got to the office. My computer was painfully slow to start like it was trying to quit the day already, and the office was quiet as people got into their work.

The thing that made this morning different from the rest, was that this morning my boss asked me to come into his office because he had an assignment for me.

"John?" I ask as I knock and poke my head around the door.

"Yes, Matthew, please come in and close the door."

It was my third year in the job, I started as a graduate and have started working my way up the hierarchy within the organisation. I was originally training to be a soldier in the Air Force, but a rough night in an outback pub swiftly put an end to that. Probably for the better seeing how often my brother in the SAS is deployed, leaving his young family behind.

I've always had an interest in the intelligence field, my Dad was in the army and my brother is part of the Special Air Service, the drive to serve my country has always been there. Heck, even my sister has a government job as a teacher in a semi-rural school. If I couldn't serve in the field, then I may as well serve behind a desk.

I was curious about being called into John's office as it didn't happen often. The question of an assignment is even less often. I wondered what bullshit he might be pulling, with me being one of the younger people in the Sydney office. I did not doubt that it was something like showing a high school kid some of the unclassified work to get them interested in the organisation, or I don't know, rescuing a cat from a tree because the fire department is too busy.

"Matthew, I've asked you in here today because we've been asked to keep an eye on a newly minted New South Wales member of Parliament."

I mentally took note of a few of the questions that came up from this opening line.

Which member? Why? What's the threat level? Why me? Is this someone in my area that I might have voted for? Could there be a conflict of interest?

"You'll have seen the news from New Zealand," John continued and I nod, "about the Dagestani individual who leaked some fairly sensitive information about New Zealand's political operations, alliances and most importantly, weaknesses to the Kremlin. Well, the New South Wales Parliament just elected a Russian-born woman and have asked us to watch over her in case this turns out to be a Russian spy nest."

"A babysitting job?" I retort, not able to hold back my incredulous tone but also thankful that it wasn't a candidate I voted for.

I didn't pay a lot of attention to the recent election except to follow the law and vote. I would have remembered if a candidate in my very suburban part of Northern Sydney anything was other than deeply, almost stereotypically, Australian.

"Simply put? Yes. We're aware she has an upcoming trip to Moscow and regularly has contact with a friend who works in the Russian Consulate. I would prefer to avoid any leaks or sensitive information getting out of course, though my gut feeling is that this is an overreaction from the New South Wales Parliament. Perhaps you can find a way to test this theory," he said with a quirk of his eyebrow. Challenging me to find something with this case.

"You think? Could I not just be paired up with some high school kid that's been touted as a genius, or you know, do cyber surveillance on this target?"

"Matt, I know you have a complete disdain for politicians of any elk, but an order is an order. You of all people should be able to respect that. The Prime Minister of Australia, despite my personal thoughts about him, has gotten a bit flighty about any kind of risk with any Eastern European in a position of political power. They've got eyes on a Polish man in Victoria and a Ukrainian in Queensland. Both of whom aren't directly Russian but have closer ties back to the ex-Soviet State and the current Russian government than Miss Zaitseva does. Think of this more as an opportunity to prove yourself to the higher-ups. Do this and I can consider you for much more serious cases."

He slipped a file across his desk to me.

"Here's her file and everything I managed to have Simon find in an afternoon yesterday. Again, I don't suspect she's anything nefarious, but we need to keep an eye on her for the next three months at least. Please spend a week watching from afar, next Tuesday she will be called back into her speaker's office and you'll have formal introductions then. Until such a time, you are her invisible shadow. That's all Matthew, you can go back to your desk now."

And like that I was dismissed with some Russian woman's deeply personal information in my hand, expected to know the woman inside and out before the week's end, then be her in-house babysitter for a few months. It honestly feels a tad nightmarish, but I suppose it could be worse.

At least I'm not in the Middle East like my brother, dealing with the blistering hot heat, and the even hotter temper of radicals shooting his way. You'd think after his second deployment finishing early due to a bullet wound, he would have stayed home, but the stubborn mule just went back. Signing up for the next deployment once the doctor gave him the okay to go back into service, despite his family's insistence to stay home and get something like an office job with the defence force.

We all knew it wouldn't suit his disposition. He was a daredevil child and hadn't changed. Our father's death from injuries sustained in action just strengthened his resolve to serve and protect Australia in every way he could.

It was instilled in all of us Taylor children years ago. Dad served in the army. Mum was a medic before she stayed home to be a housewife. The oldest son, the pride of his parents, became an elite soldier. The only daughter became a schoolteacher near where Dad was based for the longest. Then there was me.

Seemingly a disappointment to my family with my 'cushy' office job in Sydney. I'm not meant to tell anyone I work for the ASIS unless they've been cleared for it, as the ASIS is the Australian equivalent of the CIA.

But here I am.

Sighing I slumped down at my desk, and I flicked open the folder and was met with a photo of a stunning woman, albeit a bit bookish. She mustn't be shy because she's run for parliament, but the girl could have gone modelling. She looked tall, though that could be because of the camera angle, slender with soft brown curls falling to her waist. A slim waist with shapely hips, and her curves were delectable. She has an hourglass shape I knew my sister would kill for. Her features were soft, feminine Chocolate coloured eyes set in a determined stare looking down the camera lens, high cheekbones, and a button nose.

Pouty lips are the final thing I notice on her face, and I briefly wondered what it might be like to press my lips to hers to see if they're as pillowy and soft as they look. No, Matt. Wrong head. I shook that idea from my mind and read her file.

Subject: Mikhaila (Misha) Ivanevna Zaitseva
(Михаила Зайцева | Mik-haila Zayt-seva)

Born in Moscow on 27 August 1989.

Father, Ivan Zaitsev, was a farmer during the Soviet Era but in later letters to his mother (Anna, still based in Moscow) shows that he complained of the city becoming too crowded and filled with 'men seeking wealth over humanity' so moved to Vladivostok in 1991.

The family financially struggled for nine years as Ivan was a sole income earner as a fisherman before moving the family to Bondi Sydney in June 2000.

Mother, Valeriya Lepyokhina, was an administrative assistant prior to her marriage and became a homemaker once the first child of two was born.

Brother, Konstantin (Kostya) Zaitsev, was also born in Moscow. He is three years older than Mikhaila and is a well-respected chef in Bondi, known for his traditional Russian meals that are popular with Russian expatriates in the community. He owns a restaurant in Bondi called Dom, 'Home' in his native language.

Miss Zaitseva lives in an apartment in Rose Bay and the rest of her family reside in their family home in Bellevue Hill.

Mikhaila does not have many close friends, except a Miss Alexandra (Sasha) Komarova, whom it

23

seems she had met at university in their undergraduate years.

Alexandra is currently working towards a PhD in international business. Mikhaila has a master's in public policy and governance.

She is not very active on social media in a personal sense, she has never had any issues with the crown, the Australian Tax Office or any Police department and received citizenship in 2008 alongside her family with no visa complications. She currently holds both a Russian and Australian passport.

We want to confirm that she is not a threat to Australia or New South Wales by observing her for an extended period of time. The Prime Minister of Australia is dealing with approximately ten individuals from Eastern Europe in a similar situation to Miss Zaitseva (being elected to power) in Australia and these cases vary from state to state, including the federal parliament as well. As you will be aware, this all became known from a case of espionage from an Eastern European in New Zealand. New Zealand officials have advised that there are indications that this event is not contained within their borders.

We need to clear Miss Zaitseva's name in order for her to continue in her chosen career.

We predict this case will take less than a year, but we need to be thorough and make sure there is no risk to Australia, its secrets, or its people.

There were other bits in the file, a picture from Misha's graduation, her citizenship ceremony, and the opening of her brothers' restaurant.

There was a copy of her application to run as a politician, her car purchase, and a photo of her apartment before it was leased to her.

It felt a little like a violation being able to gather all this information on a person in an afternoon, but it is a part of the organisation. I have no doubt Simon, one of our junior analysts for Cyber Security, could have dug up much more if we had given him more time.

I took the time to clear up the rest of my loose ends preparing to be on this case for up to a year. I grabbed the case file and left the office for the day, preparing to sit in my Mazda CX-5, the most popular car for metropolitan areas of Australia, for the next few days.

Chapter Five – Misha

I pulled up to Konstantin's restaurant "Dom" with the best bottle of Russian vodka I could find at my local liquor store.

"Kostya!" I called as I opened the door. It was early afternoon, after the lunch service but before the dinner service, so he should be prepping for the next meal, so the dinner rush is less, well, rushed.

"Mishutka, I'm in here" he replies back at me from the kitchen.

Of course, he uses the boys' nickname for my name. We had a joke that Dad really wanted two boys, and had his sights set on the masculine version of my name. Mama only gave in to his incessant pleading to make my name Mikhaila when she bargained to allow herself to dress me in girly clothes as I grew up. It was one of my little Russian secrets. I was grateful the kids in my high school hadn't found out and being the only Russians in our school at the time, we flew under the radar. I was mocked at my school in Vladivostok though. Kids can be cruel. No matter the country.

I wander through the chairs on tables ready for the floor to be cleaned between food services and spot his mop of chestnut brown hair pulled back into a tight man bun, his back to me while he scrapes down the main stove. He looks up from his job as he sees me, and smiles.

The smile drops as he takes me in and sees the vodka bottle.

"Mishutka, you're not really a drinker. What's the occasion for..." he pauses, reading the label.

"Is that what I think it is? Misha. Good vodka?" He mocks a horrified look on his face that quickly turns to pity. I tend to prefer a crisp white wine to a vodka tonic, but times call for me to embrace my Russian roots it would seem.

"Kostya, if you want the full story, you're going to need to take a seat and find cover for prep. Because I will require a few glasses of this," I hold the vodka up, " to get through it all without crying." I had always been a sensitive soul, with a tough exterior, thanks to years of bullying, which had prepared me with a thick skin for a political role, but as soon as I was in the presence of my family, my armour comes off and I become vulnerable, like the little girl I was when we first moved to Australia.

Kostya set me up in his office, the room to do all the ordering and admin of the restaurant with two chilled glasses with ice, a touch of tonic water and a lemon wedge. He left again to sort out his restaurant, to find cover for his prepping position but was back within 15 minutes and pulled up a chair ready to hear why his baby sister was upset.

"Okay Mishutka,' he says sinking into a chair, relief to be off his feet evident on his face. "Are we celebrating again already? Or is this a commiseration?" he asks, looking at me concerned, brows drawing together and then his left eyebrow crooked up. " Do I need to shake someone down? Threaten them with a gruff Russian accent?"

I snort at that comment. Of course, he'd pretend to be a Russian mobster to scare someone on my behalf, the same way he used to do when boys hassled me at high school and university.

My brother wasn't small by any means. Standing tall at 6'2" he was built broadly helped by his near-religious visits to the local boxing gym. If cooking hadn't taken his heart at a young age, I have zero doubt that he would have made a great addition to a local rugby team if not playing at a regional level. He used to play and play well, in his high school years. Much to our father's annoyance. Papa would have preferred to see him play football or ice hockey, neither sport is nearly as popular in Australia as rugby or cricket.

In his chef whites, he could carve an imposing figure in a kitchen, especially when something is going wrong, and he starts to curse in Russian (words learned courtesy of our Babushka).

He has a strong jaw, always clean-shaven because of his work in the kitchen. Piercing blue eyes, they look like they could have been dipped in glacial water. He has high cheekbones, a strong nose, and an expressive brow line.

"No Kostya, at the moment that would make it worse." I launched into my story from there, explaining the drama and scandal in the New Zealand parliament, the way I was treated by the speaker of the New South Wales parliament, and the other Eastern Europeans who have been caught up in this mess.

I had finished three Vodka Tonics before I got to the end of the intense tale and Kostya stared at me slack-jawed.

"Seriously?" he exclaimed, "Khuy, dick", he muttered the curse under his breath. "Just because we immigrated from a country that has since been seen as unfriendly, that has historically been an ally when we were children..." his hand dragged down his face as he groaned at the unjust nature of the whole situation.

"You know Mama and Papa will help where they can? Is there anything they can do to help to clear your name? Is there anyone back in Russia they know who could help? Or maybe someone in the community in Bondi? You're no spy. I mean the last time you tried to be sneaky Babushka threatened to have you deported home. She doesn't like surprises that woman, does she? " He said referring to my last trip to visit her, which was meant to be a surprise before I got busy running for parliament.

Mama had to call her after my plane left the tarmac in Sydney, so Babushka didn't have a heart attack or some other kind of medical emergency. I showed up at her doorstep asking for lodging, giving her just a day's warning. Needless to say, surprising my very regimented grandmother was not my best idea. I groaned at that. Surprise visits to Russia will never happen again. Ever. I was put in the hot seat for every tea party Babushka hosted while I visited, and my brain hurt from translating the Babushka's gossip at speed, along with making sure there wasn't the need for more tea or sweets.

"No, Kostya. I don't think there's much to do. I'm suspended with pay at the moment pending the outcome of an investigation. I needed a sounding board to vent to, Spasibo, thanks. I'm not even quite sure what the next step for all of this even is." I huff and take another sip, finishing my hopefully last vodka tonic.

Konstantin eyes me warily. He is one of the people who knows me the best, almost better than I know myself, that no matter how I portray myself to the outside world, I'm still that shy, scared little girl who moved from Russia. I'm still the Zaychik of the family.

"Misha," my brother starts quietly, "I need to get back out there to help finish up for dinner prep. We've got a few big families booked for tonight and I want to make their experience incredible. Have you got a way to get home?"

"Da," I reply. Knowing that I'm just going to grab an Uber, order in and watch a copious amount of trashy reality television shows in my fluffiest pyjamas.

I gathered my things up, knowing that my apartment was going to be cold and lonely. Sasha said earlier she was working late at the embassy, and I didn't want to bother my parents. I wouldn't have the chance of company.

"I'll see you later Misha?" Kostya looks at me with his big blue eyes, concern plain on his face, eyebrows drawing together, wrinkling his usually flawless forehead. He knows how long I've wanted this job, and it was all ripped away in a matter of weeks.

"Da Kostya. And I'll call Mama and Papa when this whole thing is a little less... Fresh. I don't want them to worry, I don't want you to worry. I don't want to worry anyone!" I explain arms going up, "I just need to have a good night's sleep and wake up tomorrow ready to tackle this thing to the best of my abilities."

"That's it Misha!" he says slapping my shoulder. "We will talk soon. But you look after yourself, da?"

I nod and then look down at my phone as my fingers quickly find their way to order an Uber.

I look at my brother and say "I'll be out of your hair in five minutes. I'll move the chairs back in the meantime to help, then I'll relax at home."

Kostya grabbed me in one of his famous bear hugs.

"You know I love you Zaychik? Please be okay."

Concern marred his beautiful face, and I hate that I caused this.

I squeezed him back, my way of promising that I would get through this. I've survived worse.

Chapter Six - Misha

I've been called back into the Speaker's office.

To say that I am nervous is an understatement.

I hardly slept last night as my mind worked overtime catastrophising and running through the 'what ifs'. If our old immigration therapist heard this, I have no doubt she would know I'm catastrophizing.

I've been following the scandal, and the accused man was jailed in a New Zealand maximum security prison before he was able to get on a flight out of the country. Going back to Russia or one of Russia's friendly countries was impossible due to there being no direct connections between Wellington, New Zealand's capital city, and anywhere in China or Europe. His name was dragged through the mud by the media, who did a seriously impressive deep dive into Russo-New Zealand relations but also into the man's background.

Some are saying he's a hero on message boards, but many in the country are now vilifying people who speak in an Eastern European accent because of his actions. This is something I fear for my own community here in Sydney. If someone recognises my accent, but not me, I've had to lie and say I am German.

That seems to appease most people, but I am still a little concerned about what the speaker, Robert Peterson, has bought me in for.

I haven't been out of my apartment much in the last couple of weeks preferring to take comfort in the embrace of my weighted blanket, a good cozy mystery series and so many cups of tea. I've not really left except for trips down to Coles and Dymocks, Konstantin visited me though, probably to make sure I was eating properly. I've just been holed up avoiding people, so I don't get any strife from the public.

There are already murmurings online questioning how this event in New Zealand might affect Australian politics. My name hadn't specifically been bought up in Australian media, but I felt it was only a matter of time.

Wiping my palms down the front of my pants, I tentatively knock on Roberts' door, hoping for the best, but preparing for the worst.

"Come in!" he shouted through the door, a typical greeting from Robert.

He knew I was coming in today, undoubtedly, he has a couple of lines up his sleeve about how he knew he could never trust a Russian or some other thinly veiled Russophobia bullshit.

"Hi Robert," I say opening the door and peering my head through the gap. "You wanted to see me?"

Robert wasn't alone. A tall muscular man was standing beside him but with his back to me, facing out the window. From what I could see, his hair was styled back, top-heavy but contained and was standing in a stance that screams of military complete with his hands clasped behind his back while he watched the street.

My gut feeling was that whatever was going to happen next may not be all that pleasant. I gasped at the prospect of things going wrong for me. I had worked really damned hard to get to this point and was not ready for some idiot in New Zealand to take it away from me.

"Yes, Misha. The Premier, Prime Minister and I have come to a conclusion," Robert started. I gulped, hoping it wasn't audible in the present company. I need to come across as confident, knowing that any sign of weakness would be pounced upon and likely used as an excuse to blame the guilt on.

I earned my place here, and I sure as hell wouldn't jeopardise it for my birth country. A country that wanted to be rid of us as much as we wanted to be rid of it.

"We've decided to stand you down, suspend you from Parliament..."

"But sir!" I cried out, realising he wasn't finished, I bit my tongue so hard I tasted the coppery tang of blood as I realised what I had done. The Speaker was notoriously harsh on those who had outbursts when Parliament was in session. It's safe to assume that a one-on-one meeting would have a similar outcome if not worse.

"Misha." He sighed, plainly exasperated with my outburst.

"If you'll allow me to continue," he glared at me then, and I pursed my lips and nodded meekly.

"These kinds of suspensions are happening in government, at the State and the Federal level, this is happening across all levels in Australian democracy, all over this fair country. I want to make it clear you're not being singled out. This is not because of anything you have done as such. This has come from the Prime Minister who was feeling heat and pressure to act from the press."

"Okay so, in saying that. You are suspended from state parliament for the next six months or until we can clear your name, whichever comes first. This is with full pay because we aren't saying it is anything you've done, it is because of the actions of another individual in another country."

"With that, you did offer to allow us to monitor you closely. So, we will be monitoring your phone, including your apps, search history and messages. During this investigation, you've also been assigned the lovely Agent Matthew here."

"He is your shadow. He will also be moving into your apartment; we know you have the space. Frankly, New South

Wales doesn't want to fork out for the cost of the apartment next to yours so he can keep an eye on you while you're off doing whatever on the government's dime. If anyone becomes suspicious, then explain it's a relationship. I've been assured this young man is a capable actor." He waves a hand at the bored man next to him, as the man I assume to be Matthew turns around.

"He is the master of your fate, his reports each month will determine if you are coming back to parliament or if we're going to ship you back to Russia." Robert finishes his little speech and pushes Matthew towards me. If Matthew didn't choose to move, I know there would have been nothing Robert could do about it.

"Hi, I'm Matthew, but you can call me Matt", he says thrusting his hand out towards me. I don't take it, just as a general rule I don't like to shake people's hands or be super close to others unless I'm required to act in a professional capacity which because I'm feeling bitter, is not today. That and my hand is still healing after all the handshakes from businessmen in my area trying to prove their strength by squeezing the shit out of my hand when we meet. He doesn't look offended or put out when I don't shake it, I nod at him, and he drops his hand.

"I'm to accompany you, move in with you, and generally keep an eye on you. Any reports I provide will be going back to my boss at the ASIS, not Robert," he smirks then at my not-so-subtle wince. Obviously, my disdain for the speaker wasn't lost on him.

"So, if that's all Robert, I'd like to get settled into the role as Mikhaila's shadow." He looks at Robert, who dips his chin in a nod and just like that we're dismissed from the office.

Matthew grabs me by the elbow, guiding me, with me still a little dumbfounded at the way events just played out, he leads me out of the office and out of the building onto a busy but sunny street.

"Where'd you park your car?" He asks leading the way. We stop, him staring at me with a quizzical look on his face and I look up at his face, I'm now realising I hadn't really looked at this man properly.

Couldn't they assign me to someone who wasn't a model in his spare time? Or if he didn't model, could model in his spare time.

His skin was sun-kissed; his raven-black hair styled back from his face. A strong jawline, and green eyes. Forest green, a forest I could get lost in like the ones in Russia from when I was a child...

"Miss Zaitseva??" He asks, snapping me out of my blatantly checking him out. He smirks when he realises the effect he has on me and I can feel my cheeks heat in embarrassment.

"Mikhaila. That look? The one where you think I'd give up my career for a night with you. Yeah, that's not happening."

I purse my lips at his insinuations, as he continues.

"I know I'm handsome, my mother likes to remind me. So please Mikhaila, where. have. you. parked. your. car?"

I was pissed at his assumption of me. I mean he's not wrong, I was enjoying the view of him, but rude. As if I'd give him something that no one else has ever had before, giving him a part of me.

"Agent... Matthew." I realised at that point; that I didn't know his last name. Which strikes me as odd. Don't most of these kinds of guys go by their surname? Unless Matthew is his surname. I ponder on that for a minute before I remember I need to respond.

"I don't own a car. I use public transport more often than not. When I drive, it's using a rent-by-the-hour vehicle. You'd know that if you had done a proper background check. It's part of my policies as well if you look at anything I published..."

I was cut off as he started dragging me towards a silver CX-5 Mazda. These vehicles are common in my suburb, though the number plate does appear to be quite familiar.

I rack my brain trying to think about why that might be, but quickly give up, I just sit back and enjoy being driven around.

Chapter Seven - Matt

This woman. The first few days I spent staking her apartment out were a waste of time and resources. Honestly, I should have just put up a camera on the street and waited until she left the building. The first week she had two visitors, a male and a female. The male looked a lot like her, and once I had done some googling and asked Simon for photographs of her inner circle and family, I discovered it was her brother, the semi-famous-in-Sydney chef.

The other was Alexandra. Again, only an assumption but I was told she had a very small inner circle, which struck me as being a bit odd. She was a politician after all. Isn't it her job to make friends with people?

She left, walking to the supermarket for groceries once but otherwise choosing instead to have them delivered. She also received quite a few Amazon packages. I was tempted to impersonate one of the delivery kids who came and went just to see her, and see her, see what I could read off her body language in a short space of time. But I knew that would blow my cover as soon as she met me in person. One particularly miserably cold and wet day she left the apartment and went for a walk down the local beach.

I followed her in my car, her long hair was clipped back in a claw clip, only noticeable as the wind blew back her black rain jacket hood. Her slender figure wasn't made for this kind of weather, though I suppose this was one way for her to go unnoticed. No one else was game enough to brave this kind of weather. The wind was lashing the waves, which crashed violently against the wet sand, with any sand that hadn't been drenched by the downpour being lashed up into a frenzy.

She walked slowly down the empty bay. No soul was in sight, and battering against the wind and rain she must have been miserable out there. She sunk down on the wet sand, lowered her hood which kept up losing the battle against the wind, and stared out over the bay towards Sydney's famous harbour. She brings her arms up and wraps them around her knees. Her shoulders start to shudder, not from the cold, but as she gave into her emotions, and allowed tears to fall.

I wanted to leave my car and pull her into a hug. I wanted to comfort her. A human want, rather than something I could actually do. I felt drawn to her and I wanted to comfort her like I would my younger sister, but I knew I couldn't go to her, and pretend I was a stranger and check if she was okay. Yet again, it'd blow my cover. She needs to feel her feelings on her own terms.

The second week of my watch, she actually left the house, she met Alexandra at the Bondi Junction Queensgate. Following her quietly, and in disguise, I watched her have coffee, and go to Kmart and Dymocks before jumping back on the bus back to her apartment. I find it strange that it's reported that she owns a car but doesn't drive it. I dismissed the thought, thinking perhaps it was parked up at her parent's home or was getting fixed or something.

She lives a couple of floors up in her apartment block, so I was unable to watch her while she was inside, however, I did manage to set up a smart device on her door that alerts me every time it opens, again typically opening only for food or Amazon deliveries.

I gathered what I had into a report back to John.

Two weeks of watching Miss Mikhaila Zaitseva clandestinely has uncovered very little. Her inner circle comprises her brother Konstantin and her friend Alexandra. She left the apartment a total of three times over the two-week period.

The first trip was to the local Coles for groceries. The second was a walk down Rose Bay Beach in the rain. The third was a trip to Queensgate Bondi, which is where she participated in a coffee meeting with Alexandra, shopping at Dymocks and Kmart before returning on local public transport. Her brother visited a total of four times, often randomly (assuming due to the hours he keeps as a chef).

Her friend Alexandra also visited twice. Her parents have not been present, though she may have received packages from them. Further investigation would likely be more effective in a one-on-one capacity.

- Agent Matthew S Taylor.

John acknowledged the report soon after he got it and requested a meeting for me to meet Mikhaila's boss, the speaker of the New South Wales parliament.

I didn't like Robert Peterson. He came across as an arrogant ass and as if he knew better than everyone else in the room. He only restrained that attitude, especially regarding New South Wales politics when the Premier arrived to sit in on the meeting due to its sensitive nature. I was told even the Prime Minister was looking to sit in on meetings like this where meeting times worked in everyone's favour. I was thankful he wasn't able to make it today. We don't need more powerful men defining the future of women, in this case, this woman.

"So, we've done a bug sweep of Mikhaila's office," Robert started.

"And we found nothing of note in the office itself. However, on her parliamentary laptop, there was a sign of some malware whose code is similar to what we've seen out of Russia in the past."

I coughed to cover a snicker, as if this deplorable excuse for a man even knew what to do with a hammer and a nail, let alone what Russian malware code looks like.

"I want the ASIS to take possession of that laptop to conduct further in-depth analysis. I suspect my junior techs will know exactly what we're looking at if it has been seen in Australia before." My tone left no space for argument, and Robert gawked at me.

"If I may," the Premier, Karl Mitchell, started. "I would like to adhere to that request, but could your analysts come here? That way we can train our teams to learn more from your team's techniques, and make sure there is no confidential or sensitive information leaked. Not to say your technicians would ever be the cause of a leak or the like, but we don't know your office environment or how you might handle sensitive data."

I roll my eyes at that remark. Only a politician would have the balls to accuse a literal spy for the Commonwealth of Australia of leaking information.

"Sir with all due respect, you're speaking to an agent of the Australian Secret Intelligence Service. Preventing information leaks is our entire job. But we can bring someone in if that would make you feel better."

Sounds like a job for our shy Simon. He would probably hate nothing more than hanging out with pompous politicians all day who explain how things were done in their day, compared to Simon with his fancy degree from MIT. They'd claim they had better knowledge of all things tech because they've been in the industry longer, without updating themselves. It all surpasses my own knowledge of anything technical, but I can recognise talent when I see it.

"I will forward the request up to my supervisor, I doubt it will be declined," I finish, sitting back in my seat.

"Okay," Robert says, "Premier Mitchell, our other guest is due to arrive shortly, and I suspect your presence, although lovely, may cause her some alarm."

Karl Mitchell laughed heartily at that. "Well of course Robert but there's no need to be so complimentary," to which Roberts's neck starts to go a ripe shade of tomato, "I'm happy to leave with boots that aren't licked clean."

I sniggered under my breath as the Premier left. Of course, he'd pick up that Peterson was a boot-licking political climber. Both men had been in this office for the better part of the last decade.

"We have about five minutes Mr Taylor. Then Mikhaila will be joining us, and the news will be broken to her about your new involvement in the case. She doesn't need to know what happened prior..."

Peterson droned on about maintaining a sense of anonymity with Mikhaila, not to get involved with her. As he talked, I turned to face the street. It wasn't all that busy today, with a few people and cars going up and down the four-lane Macquarie Street.

I didn't hear the door open and close, but I did hear a feminine gasp and I knew Mikhaila was there.

Chapter Eight – Misha

"Good thing I have an apartment with a spare room," I say as I laugh nervously.

It had been a good few years since I had shared my space with someone and even then, I'd never shared with anyone who wasn't Russian-born.

Typically, the little apartment was a clean and tidy space. Something that was drilled into me at a young age, especially if guests are expected, not that I expected Matt to end up staying with me.

The living room is the first room you see as you come through the door. A hardwood floor is covered by a couple of well-loved rugs and my navy blue, extremely comfortable, couch covers one wall, a large panoramic print of Golden Horn Bay, just out of Vladivostok, above it.

My TV is mounted and pulled out slightly on the wall opposite the couch, with bookcases surrounding it. The bookcases are filled with romance novels and classic Russian literature. I've never had to worry about people judging my reading choices, with the more obvious romances being housed on my eReader, but I guess there's a first for everything.

It was a bit weird seeing a male in my space. I haven't really had time for relationships and even in college and high school I found it really hard to open up to guys, they all seemed to want the stereotype of a busty blonde Russian who was submissive, and my refusal to bleach my hair aside, I wasn't into that. I didn't want to be nicknamed anyone's mail-order bride, as I'd heard a few of Sasha's hookups joke between each other.

Nerves weren't the half of it. There was a gorgeous god of a man in my apartment, and I hadn't seen a guy in my living space outside of family, which frankly doesn't feel like it counts.

Fuck.

"Not that I'd mind sharing a bed," I coughed loudly almost choking on the words that had just come out of my nervous filter-less mouth. "Room, I mean room. I wouldn't mind sharing a room with you; however, I suspect you'd be more comfortable having your own space."

I gulp, hoping he doesn't mind my slip of the tongue. Maybe I just amuse him.

"Well," I say as we climb the last few stairs to my third-floor apartment and open the door with a flourish "Here we are!'.

Flustered, I ushered Matthew into the apartment.

Unfortunately, the space wasn't tidy today, politics had turned my life into a whirlwind, and housekeeping had become a casualty.

"Sorry about the mess," I muttered and grimaced as I started shoving the clothes scattered around the living room into a basket, which had also been strewn across the floor.

"Campaign life, followed closely by being accused of espionage isn't exactly conducive to tidying."

He chuckled a warm sound that calmed my apprehension at having him in my space. "Looks like you've been busy."

Busy was an understatement. I explained the long hours, community meetings, and fundraising events, the exhaustion tinged with a thrill of purpose. I flitted over the depressive episode that the accusation brought on, where getting out of bed was way too hard, harder than it should have been, and not just because it felt like the rug had well and truly been pulled out from under me.

I was starting to feel a little bit better. There are less what ifs for me to deal with.

My kitchen is to the left of the living room and is also one of the tidiest places in the house. I typically pride myself on keeping the floor clean enough to eat from, not that I would, but it was something small. But this room wasn't spared from my wallowing. Dishes cover the marble counters, and knowing the dishwasher was acting as a pretty kitchen sculpture at the moment, I hadn't emptied it in the last couple of weeks, take out had become my go-to.

My fridge was empty of food, but it was covered in memories. Postcards from Babushka, photos from Kostya's opening night, and a couple of photos of Sasha and me. One from a random party, and another from our joint trip to Russia that her father paid for when we finished our undergraduate studies. Thankfully the one thing that needs to stay clean I've kept wiped down.

The espresso machine sits in the corner of my kitchen, shining in an almost mocking way when you compare it to the rest of my kitchen.

I moved quickly across the room to put all the dishes I'd left unwashed into the dishwasher and moved all the washing into my room. I poked my head into the spare room to check it was in guest-worthy order.

I groaned as I opened the door to my guest room. Of course, I couldn't even keep one room tidy. The campaigning really had done a number on my usually tidy little apartment.

The room was strewn with posters from my campaign and many, and I mean too many, newspaper cut-outs that I was going to send back to my Babushka. The bedspread wasn't pulled up and in a crumpled state from nights I ended up sleeping in here, too tired to even move from this room, fifty steps to my own bed. I hear a noise behind me and jump.

"Gah!" I gasp. Momentarily forgetting that I'm sharing my personal space with a complete stranger. Someone who is tasked with watching me.

"I'm so sorry Matthew, I forgot to clean this up and well. Please, help yourself to a cold beer while I tidy this up."

He cocked an eyebrow at me with that.

"What?"

"Do you know if I even like beer? If I even drink?"

"You are a warm-blooded Australian-born male, right?"

He snickers at that, "Yes, yes, I am. But I'll pass on the beer, thanks. I don't drink."

"Okay suit yourself, but I'll be having a vodka soda once I tidy this mess up." Knowing that the vodka I took to Konstantine's was still in the freezer.

 He nods and turns back towards the kitchen to grab a chair to watch me clean and tidy the room.

I might be regretting not letting Sasha clean when she visited a couple of weeks ago. She'd make sure I wouldn't wallow like I have. I suspect that's why she said the coffee at Queensgate was non-negotiable. Forcing me to leave my house. I mentally kick myself for being 'lazy' knowing I wouldn't have had the heart to clean, when everything was up in the air and feeling a bit hopeless.

It took some time, but I finished tidying, put on new sheets for the bed that looked like it'd be too small for this beast of a man and allowed him to ask questions about me, my family, and my political dreams.

I finished tidying in the living room by straightening photos on the bookshelf, a framed picture of Babushka and me in front of St Basils, Moscow caught my eye.

A pang of homesickness hit me. "She'd have my head for this mess," I said, gesturing at the state of the chaos remaining. "My family doesn't tolerate untidiness like this."

Matthew's gaze softened. "Tell me about them," he said. "Your family, I mean."

I launched into stories of my mischievous older brother, the undeniable pull of my grandmother's cooking, and the unwavering support of my parents. With each word nostalgia washed over my skin, and a forgotten warmth rekindled in my chest, while a chill reminding me of a winter breeze in Russia, skated across my skin.

Chapter Nine - Misha

The biting cold of Russia seeped into my bones, a constant companion in my earliest memories. It was the kind of cold that lingered even by the fire. Perhaps that's why I remember my Dedushka the way that I do - cold and distant.

He wasn't close to Papa, and Babushka, my grandmother, seemed to blossom after his passing soon after we moved across the country. I think she loved him, but his nature meant he was holding her back. She had more capacity to love and act less like a stoic Russian housewife once she was let go of his iron grip on her life.

We lived in a cramped Brutalist-styled apartment building, common during that era, on the outskirts of Moscow. Mama stayed home to raise Kostya and me, while Papa laboured as a farmer on the outskirts of Moscow City.

Sometimes, they'd leave us with Babushka and Dedushka for "grown-up time". Those nights used to be my favourite. I would curl up next to a heater, as Babushka cooked us a hearty Stroganoff, the scent of the beef simmering and the rich earthy smells coming off the stove was enough to make all our bellies rumble in anticipation. Dedushka used to leave us be, preferring to sip vodka neat and read a book in his study than spend time with his messy grandchildren.

He still felt this way even during our last visit to Moscow before we moved to Australia. Unbeknown to us children on that visit our parents were travelling to Sydney to get everything organised for us to move there a few weeks after our return to our home.

We got off the plane, as unaccompanied minors, and stepped out into the balmy 23-degree day, a few degrees warmer than what we had left behind in Vladivostok. Because Kostya was now a teenager he was tasked by our parents to navigate the public transport network and get us safely to our grandparent's home in our old apartment block. I watched out the window in our hour-long train/bus ride and marvelled at just how much the city had changed in the few short years since we moved away from it, like flowers blooming after a long cold winter.

Older buildings were being restored to their former glory and new office buildings were popping up. Kostya was so excited when we made it to our old apartment building he gave me all our luggage and he shot out to the courtyard to meet with some old friends he had when we were living here.

I was more excited to see our grandparents, spend some time people-watching in the Red Square with Babushka, and find a good read in the local library. Dedushka always spent time at home, he wasn't very social was how my Babushka explained it to me as a child, he was sick and couldn't see other people.

I just thought he was a grumpy old man who blamed his problems on others. Kostya and I always were glared at whenever we made any kind of mess, and when Babushka was out he completely ignored us and expected us to sit and read quietly.

I was eleven when I last saw him and back then, while I liked reading, I didn't like being told to read.

Even as a young child, I sensed change on the horizon. I was young during the fall of the Soviet Union. Kostya was nearing school age, and Papa disapproved of the increasingly wealthy children our Moscow neighbours were raising.

We weren't like the families who prospered after the fall of the Soviet Union, nor were we the ones who fell into complete disarray. But within eight months, Papa decided he'd had enough. He packed the car and left with our things to set up the family home. A month later we got word from him saying he had a job, organised a good school for Kostya and we embarked on a journey across the vast country in a train with only a suitcase each. Leaving Moscow behind for a new life in Vladivostok.

The move was scary for my three-year-old self. I only knew Moscow, my grandparents, and the parks we played in. As a young girl, I had to demonstrate bravery and embrace the new adventure. Babushka made me remind her that while it was a big move, it would all be okay because I was her Zaychik. I knew Konstantin was anxious as he had to start school on top of the move, held back because Papa didn't want him in school in Moscow. I knew Mama was nervous because she wanted the best for us children but hadn't ever left Moscow herself. She hadn't needed to. I held my fear back, so I didn't worry Mama further, especially during the multi-day train trip. She had her hands full with Kostya and me.

Vladivostok was colder as far as the weather went, but the people were warmer. It felt less like a big concrete city and more like a home. Papa got a job as a fisherman, and this meant he was sometimes out to sea for weeks on end. I knew this left Mama feeling lonely, and Kostya and I tried to be as good as we could when he was away. Sad Mama was the worst thing to see as a child. We knew she cried herself to sleep the first few nights Papa was away.

Every time.

My memories of Vladivostok were of family holidays hiking in the forests around Amur Bay, of finding high points together and foraging for mushrooms to accompany dinner and berries to consume on the way home. Or visiting the islands to the south of Vladivostok where we went with Papa on one of the fishing boats.

In summer, though they were short, we swam, in winter we cosied up next to the fireplace because we finally had one. There is nothing like the smell of a woodfire and spiced hot chocolate in the evenings.

Something that still reminds me of the Vladik winters.

We spent seven years in the pretty red brick house near the ocean, a happy family until my father lost his job suddenly just after the turn of the century and we had to move again. This time out of Russia. An even scarier prospect for a pre-teen me.

The first thing I noticed about Sydney was the accent. How everyone spoke English. I wasn't used to it, I used to watch cartoons from the West growing up, but they were all American. And the Australian accent was much different. I was taught to speak British English in my primary school, so thankfully I didn't struggle with the language like my parents did to begin with.

But my thick Russian accent stuck. It caused me to speak more softly because I didn't want to call my accent to attention, and over time it did soften but I will always sound 'Russian' to Australians. I was teased for being quiet. At school, it confused me, teased for my accent but also teased for being quiet, caused by the teasing from my accent. I couldn't win. It was okay when my brother and I were in the same school, no one wanted to mess with the big Russian rugby forward, but as soon as he left and went to culinary school I was left to my own devices, left to defend myself.

Mama and Papa didn't understand why the children at school had been so mean, but in phone calls back to Russia, Babushka got it. That meant the world to me.

To feel heard and understood. If it wasn't for her, I may have given into the boy's advances, wanting to know what the hype around Eastern European girls was (even though I didn't live in that part of Russia for long) based almost completely on what they watched in porn. I may not have retained my dignity through high school and kept that focus through my university years if it wasn't for Babushka's unwavering support and wise words.

I also realise it makes me strange in a sense, someone my age, straight but not having much experience with men.

I finish with a blush, realising what I had just said out loud to Matt. Self-awareness was a blessing and a curse.

"Um. I'm sure you didn't want to know that, or needed to know that about me" I say awkwardly, the flush of a blush creeping up my neck.

"I like that you're honest Mikhaila, there aren't enough honest people in the world. Certainly not in your field of work typically." Matthew responded chuckling.

"Misha. My full name is Mikhaila, but Misha is the definitive form in Russian, like a nickname. I'm only really called Mikhaila when I'm in trouble."

"Misha it is then," he responded with a smile.

"We should probably consider some dinner and then bed huh? I'll get onto cooking something." I say as I bustle out of the spare room towards the well-stocked kitchen, feeling like a weight was lifted off my chest from talking about my past.

Chapter Ten - Misha

Matt and I pulled up to the restaurant in Matt's car, knowing there was no way I would get rid of my shadow tonight. Annoyance swept over me as I jumped out of the car, him closely following behind me. Like sure buddy, I'm your case, but I do need a bit of breathing space at times.

Sasha learned about what happened in New Zealand after we had a coffee the other week. She was horrified at the treatment the Dagestani man received and demanded an urgent and non-negotiable dinner attendance once she finished work the next day.

"I don't understand why they would imprison him. Why not just deport him back to Russia?" She cried.

I glanced towards the front of the restaurant; we were seated at the back for privacy. I asked Konstantin to do so, Matt sat at the front of the restaurant and thankfully Kostya and Sasha were chatting so didn't see us arrive out of the same vehicle. On top of all of that drama, I really didn't want to lie to Sasha or Kostya and claim something like a random ride-share situation and then be asked a million and one questions about the gorgeous Australian man I showed up at the same time as.

Matt at his table for one, reading a book and sipping on a glass of water. He was picking at the food in front of him that I knew Kostya would have made and chosen specifically to help make the typically Australian man expand his palette.

"Sasha," I started, using a more hushed tone with her. I knew we were safe in Dom as it was known as the 'Russian' hangout spot, but I still didn't want her drawing extra attention to our table and our conversation.

"How could they have possibly sent him back to Russia? What if he knew information about that Government that he could only say in person to his handler in The FSB or SVR? The New Zealand Government couldn't possibly risk that. I'm just personally aware that he's the second New Zealand citizen to ever be charged with espionage."

"Wait. Only the second? Did the USSR not conduct spying operations in New Zealand during the Soviet period?"

"Apparently yes, but they fled before the government was able to lay any charges."

Sasha moved on from that topic thankfully. I didn't feel the need to tell her that I had done a lot of googling around foreign interference, and what had happened in New Zealand and Australia. I learnt more about what I and other Eastern European figures had been accused of, and what the outcome might be for any one of us who have been accused if we were found guilty somehow. The implications of being charged with espionage could be anywhere from life in a maximum-security prison to a minimum of 10 years. I don't understand why anyone would risk that kind of time unless they were sure they could get away with it. Or why they'd pledged themselves to serve one government by betraying another. This kind of betrayal just doesn't add up in my head.

"Misha?" She asked, dragging me out a panicked thought of what if I was found guilty, even if I hadn't done anything to warrant the accusation.

She eyed me, and it became very clear I had missed a question.

"Sorry Sasha, I'm a bit stressed with everything going on at the moment, and I sometimes just space out and worry."

Sasha laughs quietly at that. "Never change Misha. I swear you do the worrying for the entire state, if not the entire country."

If only she knew. I think the anxious nature of mine started back in Russia, in the Moscow days. Dedushka was a rough man, and also very hyper-vigilant. I knew he was the figurehead of the Zaitsev family. A dynasty he called it, and I know my father hates our family being referred to like that still.

I am pretty sure our family moving to Australia was the last straw for my Dedushka, He died not long after, freeing Babushka from his iron rule. She disclosed, that back in prewar Russia, they had an arranged marriage. A way to bring two relatively well-off families together. It hadn't gone all that well, and my understanding was that Dedushka lost a lot of money when Russia became the USSR and he fell out of favour with the government. He was always bitter towards his loss and blamed Babushka for it in part.

"I'm sorry Sasha, I'm probably terrible company tonight. I just can't help but worry about the what-ifs. I worry if I'm going to have to flee the only home I really know if they could find or fabricate a reason to find me guilty."

Sasha looked at me sympathetically.

"Have you gone back into your office since our lunch catch-up?"

I shook my head, feeling at a complete loss at what I could do about the whole situation other than wait and see. Oh and of course worry.

"Oh, Misha. I am so sorry that this is happening. Yobushki-vorobushki, *fucking sparrows*."

I rolled my eyes at her, she probably doesn't realise she's been a bit racist against other Russians, but in the social circles she grew up in, the ones my father had tried so hard to keep Konstantin and me away from, it wasn't uncommon to blame 'lesser Russians' for any woes that have come of them. I'm glad in a sense that I didn't know about these attitudes until I was older because I know I would probably been just like Sasha, and I didn't have the kind of money she had to back me up and get me out of trouble if I did get into serious trouble for insulting the wrong person.

"How are your family back in Piter?" I ask as a distraction.

Her family seem to almost run the city of St Petersburg, affectionally nicknamed Piter. Her father found himself in a position of power when he worked his way up in a steel manufacturing business from the time he was a child until he became the CEO. The fall of the Soviet Union helped him along too. He's often heralded as a self-made man, but because he has influence in the Kremlin, he has found himself in the top 100 most powerful men in Russia. Someone to avoid, and definitely not piss off.

"They're good, I think. It's been a little while since I called them." Sasha replied shaking her head.

"Has he been threatening to drag you back to Russia again Sasha?" I ask, concern lacing my voice.

Mr Komarov treated his family the same way he treated the rest of his company and people in his sphere of influence. With an iron fist and a lot of control. He has been threatening to get Sasha deported since our first year of university if her grades ever drop below a B+. Her freedom was enough to keep her (mostly) focused on her studies rather than parties and boys. When she got into the doctorate program and needed to also work while she studied, her father got her a job at the Russian Consulate in Sydney, he likely has a staffer or two there also on his pay role keeping an eye on her.

"No, which is unusual. I haven't even really heard from Mama or Maxim." She sighs. She always strived to please her family, and I know this kind of distance, both the physical and the emotional, is probably taking a serious toll on her.

"Shall we just order dessert, a final glass of Kostya's finest vodka and call it a night Misha?" Sasha asked.

"Sure," I said waving over one of Kostya's waiters. "Two Ptichye Moloko and two vodka sodas please."

He nodded and walked away with the order.

"I need to run to the lady's room quickly, I'll be back in a few minutes okay Sasha?"

She nodded, and I excused myself to the lady's room. Much like everything else at Dom, it felt like home. Kostya had modelled everything in the restaurant after our home in Vladik, complete with the bathroom mimicking the one we had back there, with little touches like our childhood height measurements in Cyrillic on the wooden door frame, much like the one we had back in Russia. My fingers flittered over the measurements, remembering the excitement of getting measured, every season without fail, and seeing who was taller as if it was a race between Kostya and myself on who could reach the heavens first. Needless to say, with Kostya being over six feet, I lost that race.

I came back into the restaurant, seeing Matt glaring towards me, and Sasha on her phone at our table. Two vodka sodas and two decadent, delicate Ptichye moloko's placed at our seats.

I sit, sip the vodka soda in front of me and tap my spoon on my plate. This causes Sasha to look up, apologies in her eyes as she dipped her cake fork into her dessert.

I followed suit, the flavours of the dessert danced across my taste buds, the softness of the sponge, coupled with a whipped mousse and a rich cocoa topping. Konstantin outdid himself.

Sasha and I finished our desserts and drinks and left separately. Sasha was being picked up by one of her father's friend's drivers, and Matt was escorting me out, being careful not to seem to be 'together' but more like two strangers who just happened to leave the same restaurant at the same time.

We got into his car, and he stared at me before starting the engine.

"What?" I asked, knowing I hadn't done any suspicious or out of the ordinary this evening. He even had my phone the whole evening so there was no way I could contact anyone or anything when I went to the bathroom.

"I don't trust her." He stated bluntly.

"Um, well excuse me. You don't really trust me either Matthew." I say with an eye roll. Of course, he can't trust a Russian.

"I don't trust you, because it's my literal job to clear your name if it can be. I don't trust her because I have a bad gut feeling. She was straight onto her phone as soon as you left the table and didn't even look up at the server when they dropped off the dessert and vodka."

"That's just Sasha, she's a 20-something, who had everything growing up so doesn't have the same kind of social graces as those of us who grew up with a lot less."

He grunted at that, which I took to mean he was satisfied with my answer as we drove back to my little apartment only a few minutes' drive away.

Chapter Eleven - Matt

It was time to send the second report on Misha to John back at headquarters. I know this is my job and we've gotten to know each other but I feel a little uncomfortable about this particular case. Maybe because we've actually gotten close as humans, where my professional boundaries have been bent out of shape a little, having to report factually back to my superior is fine I guess, but anything more than that and I might find myself in some fairly heated water.

I'd been around her for the last few weeks and I felt like I knew her well enough going into this report. Who am I kidding? I've lived with her for a couple of weeks, following her constantly with my eyes. Following those curves, those cute moments where she sings to herself when she thinks I can't hear her while making coffee for the both of us.

She had been nothing but a gracious host during my stay in her apartment and I found no major reason to be suspicious of what she had been accused of thus far.

A search conducted while she was asleep had nothing came up to incriminate her, though I did find a tracker in her purse that wasn't from the ASIS, and a bug behind one of the kitchen cabinets she didn't seem to go in much. It also didn't look like one of ours.

The boss had told me that we were going to stay on the case for another few months at least, especially as we know she has a flight booked back to Moscow, not that she's told me about it. Perhaps that should also be a red flag unless she might have thought she'd be cleared of the accusation before she took off for her grandmother's home. Then there's the thing about a record of her purchasing a car but she vehemently denies that she's ever bought a vehicle. Nothing puts Misha in a particularly bad light, though something is going on around her.

I don't expect anything to come out of the car situation, but it's important to keep the premier and the prime minister on side. It's just another job at the end of the day, right? And it gives me something to follow up on or get Simon onto when I eventually get back into the office. Simon will also get the job of trying to track back the bug I found. The tracker could still be useful, so I haven't removed it.

I sat down at her kitchen table while she walked into her kitchen to make a start on dinner for us both. I did offer to make some of the dishes I grew up with, but she told me that it would be an insult to her Russian upbringing for a guest to do any of the cooking, not that I'm complaining. My family would be the first to attest that anything I make takes me a very long while to get right.

My phone starts ringing just as my fingers hover over my keyboard, and seeing it's the office, I excuse myself from the kitchen table. Taking my laptop with me and moving into the spare room.

"Hello, Matthew speaking," I started, as the call connected, and I heard rustling in the background.

"Matt? It's Simon here, how are you going mate?"

"Good, though I'm assuming you're not calling in the evening to exchange pleasantries or chat about the weather. Especially when you've called me while I'm on assignment."

"No boss, I mean sir," he says getting flustered.

"Get to the point Simon," I say deliberately hardening my voice.

"I'm not here to fuck spiders".

"Oh yes, well we've had an update on the case you're working on. You know you said a few days back that Mikhaila doesn't drive or own a car; well, we found the car. It was found burned out on the Great Western Highway, between Bathurst and Yetholme. Local authorities thought it might just be some rowdy car enthusiasts and have since crushed the burned-out vehicle. I figured you'd want to know. Also,"

"Just a sec Simon," I say interrupting him, "I need to make a note of all of this." I grabbed a notepad from my locked bag and started scribbling furiously in shorthand and code to keep up with the information he was giving though keeping the information confidential unless the code cracker had the key to the code in my desk and could read shorthand.

This whole business with the car wasn't adding up in my mind. Something didn't feel right in my gut. Add in the tracker and the bug and my whole body tensed at the idea that this could be a set-up.

"Hey Simon, can you please send me a report on the car and include everything the local cops mentioned in it?"

"Sure boss, um the next bit…" He gulped, and I suspected whatever was coming out of his mouth next was probably not going to be something I wanted to hear, especially as I was starting to like Mikhaila as a person. She was nice, and kind. Nurturing without being overbearing and after looking after myself, my sister and Mum after Dad's death and my brother's enlistment, it was nice to have someone care for me. Well, and to remember it. I don't have good memories of my bender days where I know my family cared for me once I shattered and was broken.

"Out with it Si." I bark down the line.

"Sir, a flash drive was uncovered in Mikhaila's office."

Sighing I bite back the string of profanities I want to let loose. I settle on one.

Fuck.

"I'm sorry, Simon can you repeat that and explain the situation, slowly," I lengthen the word to get across the idea I was a bit shocked that something was uncovered that very much could complicate things for Misha.

"What would the significance of the flash drive would be in this case?" I ask him.

Simon launched into an explanation including walking me through his day in Parliament House, in Misha's office, while making disparaging remarks about how clueless the staff were. Before finally getting to the point about finding a flash drive in one of her drawers amongst a bunch of paperwork. On the flash drive was Russian Malware, which we were hoping to avoid finding should Mikhaila be found not guilty.

They couldn't determine if it had been used or not but were running those kinds of tests on her laptop. They also found that it had a transmitting function, much like a bug, which allowed whoever had created the device to hear every conversation in the office without the drive being plugged in.

It was a new and emerging technology. Something we had only heard rumours of coming out of Eastern European countries.

I hang up with Simon and curse.

Double fuck.

My full report would be less complimentary than I'd like, with the added complications Simon has just brought to my attention it's also going to take me a lot longer. I made a start regardless, including the gut reactions to all the news from Simon. I flicked John a quick message to let him know of the delay and started to gather all my thoughts and pulled out my laptop to make a start on this damned report.

Mikhaila Zaitseva hasn't done anything to draw particular attention to herself or any kind of espionage activities that she has been accused of. Her social circle remains small, her friend Alexandra and her family in Australia being her social contacts in the country, the only person she's contacting in Russia is her grandmother. After translating some of her conversations, it was evident that these were just part of her relationship with her grandmother and nothing nefarious at this stage.

However, there has come to light a few damning pieces of evidence against Mikhaila. The first was a car that she purchased and registered in her name. This vehicle was found in inland New South Wales (near Bathurst) burnt and then crushed by the local authorities. This is despite her claiming that she has never owned a vehicle. A further report about this incident is expected shortly and this should explain in more depth what happened, and I should be able to collaborate Miss Zaitseva's whereabouts at the time of the incident.

The second thing that has come to the ASIS's attention is the existence of a highly technical flash drive. This drive was filled with Russian Malware, and a letter to Mikhaila in Cyrillic, which upon translation was all nonsense, the drive also acted as a bug in her office.

During a search conducted in the apartment within 24 hours of moving in with Mikhaila, a bug was uncovered in the kitchen which I have forwarded on for further analysis. A tracking device was also discovered in Mikhaila's purse. This has been left as it could be useful in a strategic sense in the future.

This has thrown into question if Mikhaila is actually innocent, or if something else is happening. It is unclear if the flash drive was plugged into her laptop, and this has recently come into the ASIS's possession in order to thoroughly examine it for Malware.

In conclusion, I will require further time in order to ascertain Mikhaila's situation, and if she is innocent; who might be at fault?

I have also put in a request for a full report on Miss Alexandra Komarova for background and to figure out her connection to this case as a Russian national.

A further report will be provided upon my return from Mikhaila's visit to Russia.

- Agent Matthew S Taylor

"Dinners ready!" I hear Misha call down the hall. And I can't help but not only feel a bit guilty because of the news Simon gave me, and the report I have just sent to John, but I am just doing my job.

The smell of lamb dances down the hallway towards her dining room, and I am brought back to my childhood when Sunday roasts were my Mum's speciality and something all us kids longed for.

A mouthful of lamb had memories of my upbringing overwhelm me and I found myself back in the Hunter Valley.

Chapter Twelve - Matt

The final mouthful of homecooked roast lamb had its rich and distinctive flavours dancing over my tongue and I was pleased I managed to beat my brother to the final slice of the tender flavourful meat.

The whole family was around our dinner table, unbeknownst to us, this was the last time we would all be together like this. It was early in 2011, I was just out of university and getting prepared to follow the family tradition of joining the Army. My brother had completed his first training set and was preparing for a deployment and further training in Western Australia. Dad was preparing for yet another stint overseas, much to the disappointment of my mother, who after Dad was shot at last time, didn't want him coming home in pieces. My younger sister is about to start her studies as a teacher at Newcastle University in a few weeks' time. The whole family was leaving the picturesque Hunter Valley for something more. Even Mum was planning on going back to work on a local vineyard for a while Dad was deployed.

"Anyone for dessert?" Mum asks across the table, looking satisfied about the fact that she can still feed her family and keep them all happy.

We all nod enthusiastically, and Dad asks us boys out to the veranda for a beer and a breather to let dinner settle before dessert.

Opening up the screen door, Dad says "You know I'm proud of the both of you right?" his gaze going towards the horizon, the paddocks in the valley admiring the diminishing light while sipping on his beer.

My brother also gazes out over the paddocks as he nods, sipping on his own beer.

"What's brought this on Dad?" I ask, perhaps a little naïvely.

"I'm leaving tomorrow for Afghanistan. James is going to Perth next week. You're heading out to start training in a couple of months' time. I didn't know how I'd feel to see you boys follow in my footsteps like this, because as you know it's not the safest or easiest career path out there. Your mother would say I've been a bad influence on you both," he chuckles to himself at that. Because Mum would say that. She hasn't been super keen on her 'baby boys' going off to war.

"Regardless of what she says I am deeply proud of the both of you. I want the best for you, and I want you both to always do good by the family first, country second."

The mood sobered then.

"Dad, is this mission going to be more dangerous than before?" asked James looking back at us.

He was a replica of Dad. Dark hair cropped close to his skull, dark brown eyes that seemed to swallow the world when he aimed his gaze your way. He was solidly built, but a little shorter than me, stockier. I took after my mother more, with her eyes and hair, but Dad's build, Dad's hair colour and the extra couple of inches of height. Helen was a carbon copy of Mum however complete with her nurturing nature.

Dad shook his head at James, all of us knowing this could be the last time we all hung out like this regardless of what happened with Dad's mission. In war it's always dangerous, we could all be called up by our country at any point.

Only eight months had passed before everything completely and irrevocably changed.

I was on the base having finished another day of basic training and had just finished a pretty average meal in the mess hall when my major sought me out. I had a fairly good working relationship with him but we weren't close in a meaningful way.

"Have you spoken to your family today?" he asked cornering me.

"No sir?"

"Use my office. You need to call home. This is non-negotiable. An order cadet"

I raised my eyebrow at him, but he handed me the keys to his office.

"Is there something I should know?" I ask taking the keys from his outstretched hand.

He shakes his head at me, and I walk in the direction of his office. I unlocked the door and admired the systematic tidiness that the major kept in his own working space, where cadets couldn't mess things up.

I dialled home.

"Taylor household, Helen speaking."

I found it strange that my sister was answering the phone. Usually, Mum was the only one home, and even then it was unusual as she was usually out at a local vineyard conducting private tastings. Helen should be in Newcastle right now studying towards being a teacher.

"Hey Helen, it's Matt. My major told me I had to call?" I could feel the questioning in my voice, and my gut feeling was that something was really wrong.

"Mattie!" Helen sobs down the phone line and I want to reach through the line and embrace her, hold her, and let her cry out whatever she needs to cry out.

"Helen, sissy, what's wrong?" I ask. I hate hearing my family upset, but Helen being hurt really makes me feel like I'm a bit of a useless brother because I'm not there to help or comfort her. I've always fought her demons with her.

I'm her personal demon slayer. I still remember her demanding that I be the only one who could check under her bed before she went to sleep for monsters, something I held over my older brother at the time.

Something is definitely wrong. She's not naturally a crier.

I let her sob and try to get the words out.

"M-m-m-matt. We need you to come h-h-home." She says through crying-induced hiccups.

"Okay Helen, I'll come home as soon as I can. But what's happened? What do I tell my superiors?"

"Dad." She says with finality.

She couldn't stop crying so I disconnected the call and sat back in my commanding officer's seat.

Something's wrong.

Really wrong.

Dad was shipped back to us in pieces, devastating our mother, and causing Helen to move back to the valley to look after her and finish her course online the best she could. Helen struggled a lot seeing Mum so distraught. It's in her nature to fix everything. But this was something that had broken the entire family, there was no coming back, no fixing this. Helen had to put studies on hold for a trimester while working full time so that Mum didn't lose our family home in her grief. The grief threw Mum into a deep depression that took almost ten years for her to fully emerge from.

Dad died of his injuries here in Australia, and the last time I saw my older brother James was at the funeral.

Dad's death was painful and incredibly drawn out. He came home to Australia in November but didn't die from his injuries until March the next year. During 90% of that time, he was in a coma and in his final week we were told he would never wake up, and that he was completely brain dead. He had been fighting brain death the whole time, but the fight had gone out of him in the end.

It took Mum four days after she was told he was effectively dead to finally pull the plug. Us kids were numb, but the death broke her. Our grandparents were also distracted but a lot of the final preparations and arrangements were a combined effort of us kids and grandma. It was a small service. He was well-loved in the military community, but they did their own thing months ago before his final slide into his comatose state.

The doctors told Mum it was highly unlikely that he would ever wake up. Back when there was a 5% chance of him coming back, which she clung to.

The small local church was filled with lilies, causing Helen's eyes to stream with more than tears of grief. The ceremony was small, filled with memories of Dad as a civilian, but without his army friends, it did feel a little like we were missing a major part of his life.

He stated in his final will that he wanted to be cremated, but we kids and my father's own mother decided to overrule his wishes, Mum needs to be able to visit and still feel connected with him. Graves are for the living. I suspect without the grave to visit Mum might have completely broken and not made her way back to the present.

Something broke in me when we were lowering him into the ground, feeling the literal weight of him leaving my shoulders. I look up and see something also crack in my brother's eyes.

James has ever since been on a mission to get revenge against those who half blew our father up.

I'm not sure if it's revenge or madness but it took a lot of convincing for him to at least hold off going to the same region of

Afghanistan Dad had fought in. A lot of convincing to get him to drop the idea of going to Dad's old station and tracking down the rebels and executing them, committing war crimes at the very least, likely to get himself killed in the process.

When he heard the news he went into full self-destruct mode, broke off his engagement with his high school sweetheart who was also in the military, a relationship that had spanned the better part of ten years, threw himself into the hardest military academy training he could find, and went back off to war.

He worked up the ranks and managed to get into a more exclusive unit of the Air Force and was constantly overseas defending Australia.

My response to this was completely different, however. I was forced out of my military training course, mostly because of grief. But the grief manifested into a drinking problem, which resulted in a rather rowdy bar brawl in a backwater pub in rural New South Wales.

The news from the brawl made it back to my major and I was discharged from the Australian Defence Forces. At that point, to do any work that would feel meaningful and give back to Australia I needed to make a change.

I needed to get sober and go into a rehabilitation centre. Which I did. It was hard, and the detoxing process is something I wouldn't ever want to experience again. After three months sober, I went and got a tattoo of a tally of the months I spent fucked up, on the inside of my wrist over my pulse. I know others probably question it when they see a bunch of lines there but it's a daily reminder for me, a reminder of what happens when I lose control. I lose control and I risk losing everything that meant anything to me.

Chapter Thirteen – Misha

"So Matt," I say while leaning against the door frame and knocking against it lightly.

He looked up expectantly at me from where he was working on his laptop.

"Yeah?" he asks, eyebrow raised.

"I suspect you already know this, but I have a trip to Russia next week, and I'm assuming you're coming?" I ask, both dreading the response because explaining this situation to Babushka will probably hurt her, but not having Matt around would also be equally weird, Especially as he's been a constant in my life over the last 6 weeks.

"You assume correct." He states before dipping his head to look back down at his laptop and resuming his typing away. What is he even doing on that computer?

I sigh at the dismissal but then walk up to him and slap the laptop lid down, narrowly missing his fingertips, in order to get his attention. He hisses at the near miss and glares up at me.

"I know you probably don't get this a lot, but if you broke this Misha, or ever display violence towards me again, I will. Bury. You." He seethed, obviously furious that I wasn't upset about the near miss of his fingertips, or at any damage that would have occurred to his laptop. Rolling my eyes at his overreaction, I sit on the bed next to him.

"What are you doing?" he asks, eyebrow quirking. His anger quickly dissipates in his eyes to something equally as fiery.

"We need to talk about how we're going to approach this. My Babushka is very traditional. And I don't want her to think that I'm in trouble, especially with Australia. We need to come up with a good cover story." I explain.

His other eyebrow lifts, so they both reach the midpoint of his forehead before dropping, "Oh that's easy. We were told right at the beginning of this assignment, that if anyone who doesn't have the security clearance knows that you're under close observation by the Australian government, they need to think that we're dating."

I stare at him, the traditional thing obviously going well above his head, either that or we have very different meanings of the word traditional.

Traditional in my family means living apart until marriage and going to the Orthodox Russian church every Sunday.

Traditional in Australian families seems to be teenage pregnancies and family BBQs for Christmas. Maybe that's a little harsh, but you get the idea. I suspect that the word has lost its meaning for Matt.

"Babushka won't accept us to be just dating, she will interrogate you until you break, remembering she is tough as nails, unless she thinks I've accepted you fully. She also can't handle the idea that Konstantin likes men instead of women, even though he is completely free to do so in Australia. Homosexuality is all but illegal in Russia. It's why he can't come back to Russia any more. If he goes out and brings a man home for the night there is a chance that he could be arrested and jailed for five years. More recently they've deemed the LGBTQI+ movement as extremist. We're going to have to, at the very least, be engaged."

He stared at me then. "Excuse me? This wasn't part of the deal."

His reluctance took me by surprise. Does that mean he has a wife already? A partner? A fiancée? Or is he like Koysta and not like girls in a sexual way?

Does he just not like me?

Or is this just another reason for me to stress and worry incessantly?

Probably.

"Obviously it'll just be while we're in Russia. You have a cover story as well, right? Or can I come up with something that is willing to satisfy the authorities and my grandmother?" I stared up at him, pleading with my eyes as I continued.

"If we go through with this there needs to be some ground rules, and we need to be comfortable with a little public affection to make it believable."

Though the thought of kissing this god-like man made my heart race like it was election night all over again, the thought of him agreeing to this entire scheme felt kind of crazy.

He sighs, showing me that perhaps he is less than enthusiastic about his new travel buddy, I guess that's a good thing for the cardio workout my heart was currently going through.

"Yeah, it actually works better than the plan I was going with. Do you need anything to make it believable? And when did you want to, I guess 'practice', at what public affection looks like for us?" He did practice in air quotes, and again maybe I'm looking too much into it but that feels like another sign of being less than enthusiastic.

"We don't have to if you don't wa…" I couldn't finish my sentence, as he moved his hand to softly grasp my jaw, making me gasp and look at his face more closely. His eyes. They remind me of the forests my family used to hike through in Vladivostok. They had a depth to them, which signified that he had seen some haunting things. He looked my face up and down before releasing my chin and a smirk graced his face.

"Well, we will definitely need that practice, especially if grasping your chin has you gasping and flinching away."

I cringe at that, my lack of experience with men who aren't related to me is on full display. I didn't even realise I flinched, but he has a valid point. I wasn't overly comfortable with men as a general rule, but a man like Matt makes it even harder to open up. Why did he have to be so damned attractive?

I tentatively reach my hand out towards his face and brush a few loose strands of his hair behind his ear. I look up through my lashes at his face, my heart beating wildly in my chest as I consider what I'm doing.

What the hell am I doing?!

I look into his stunning green eyes and move my own face closer. It's more okay when I'm in control.

I'm less likely to be hurt or judged if it's my actions rather than his, right? I exhale through that thought.

I know I'm overthinking the whole damn thing as he brings his face in the final few centimetres and seals our lips with a passionate kiss.

I jerk back. I mean a closed-mouth kiss is nice, but I wasn't expecting him to move, and I've found all my boundaries broken.

Shit.

I pull away, feeling weird about the kiss that just happened. Not bad, just weird. He looks hurt too, like I had slapped him, his eyes downcast.

"It's not my fault Motya, I'd not had much to do with men outside of my family. I didn't want to become someone's stereotype or goal because of my nationality."

"What does Motya mean?" He asks picking up on my new nickname for him, rather than labouring on the point that I was effectively a 30-something-virgin with only a couple of kisses under her belt as far as any kind of experience with men went, and even then, I was drunk. Except for this kiss. This was my first sober kiss. And hell, I could use a drink right now to make it a less-than-sober kiss rather than freaking out like I had.

"Motya is the nickname for people with the Russian version of the name Matthew," I explain to his slowly becoming less confused face. "It is less formal, and if we're going for affection, that's a start for me."

He sighs, knowing he's not going to win that argument, and instead pulls me next to him so my butt was touching his thighs, and I could lean my back against his arm. A rush of heat goes south of my waistband, and I was a little concerned he might notice that even being close to him was a bit of a turn-on for me. I think if I hadn't flinched back the kiss would have made me more turned on than I had ever been. Maybe making me finally act on some of the urges I'm feeling.

Do I have the same sort of effect on him?

"When are we going again?" He asks quirking his head my way.

Is he trying to be cute? Does he want another kiss?

Or am I just losing my mind?

My mind. I am sure I'm overthinking everything.

Wait.

Did my breathing just speed up?

Fuck.

What was the question?

"When are we flying out?" he asked again, left eyebrow seeming to lift in mocking for my unfocused, chaotic and slightly horny mind. "Uh. Next Thursday. It'll take about 22 hours to get there, stopping in Dubai for a couple of hours."

He grunts and his arm snakes its way around my waist as he tugs me closer. I'm putty. I have melted, and have died in the arms of this gorgeous man.

"Guess we need to have a crash course on this affection thing and PDA huh?" he asks with an eyebrow quirked at me.

I gulp loudly and he loosens his grip.

"Before we go into it, you've said in the past you've not had much experience with men, or boys as the case may be," He smirks at that. As if anyone who has previously so much as touched me in a slightly suggestive manner must have been young. Or at the very least not worthy of the title, man. I mean, not wrong. But highly assumptive.

"So, what experience have you got?"

I gulp again. I know this will be mortifying, and I can already feel the shame causing any trace of arousal to dissipate and the red-hot flush of a blush creeping up my neck.

"Um. I've kissed a guy. When I was like 19, I was very drunk. It wasn't that good, and he tried to feel me up, but my brother showed up and promptly put a stop to that.

It reminded me of a plunger like he was trying to drag my tongue out of my mouth. It was gross an put me off kissing or boys for a very long time.

When I was still at university Alexandra played with my breasts." I say shrugging.

"She said it was an experiment to find out if I was interested in women, or just a bit of a prude. And turns out it was more of the prude and my sky-high standards than my liking woman. It's not that I haven't been interested in people before, I just." I say as I continue to word vomit. These are all of my deepest insecurities, and I'm telling a man whose job is literally to report my secrets back to the Australian government.

Here's hoping no one knows how to put in an SOI request about this.

"I'm just so used to the teasing and people only wanting me because I'm something different. Someone dating me could have been teased for having a 'mail order girlfriend' and I can't stand the idea of that…" I sigh. Knowing I'm over-explaining all of this and I'm probably boring him.

I sigh again and continue "So I just didn't. Not that I haven't found. Well. Sasha took me to a sex shop and told me I wasn't allowed to leave without something. So, I've explored myself a little. But ah."

I can feel my face contort into a grimace as I reveal some of my deepest sexual secrets.

"I've never asked for assistance."

I sigh again, eyes starting to well up. My cheeks were hot with embarrassment and deeply ingrained shame. Laying my secrets out there for someone to judge feels so vulnerable and I don't know if I should be trusting Matt, but my gut says he won't tease me for sharing this. I can feel myself trying to shrink back into myself, as I bring my legs up from the floor to curl up to my chest. Something to make me feel safer than I currently do, with everything stripped bare and open for him to judge.

Chapter Fourteen - Matt

"So what experience have you got?" I ask her, genuinely curious. This woman was a complete enigma to me. She's so confident but hides parts of herself away from everyone. How does she cope with it? The constant acting and shying away from tough conversations. I mean I don't think she's ever talked about her personal life in her campaign, which must have made it tough for her campaigning. She must have really resonated with her community without highlighting traditional values like having a husband or kids.

She gulps loudly and I close my laptop shifting it to the side. I shuffled over a little on the bed, to allow her some more space, but moved her across with me, so her legs hung over the side rather than her being perched on the bed. Making her more comfortable might help, right?

"Um. I've kissed a guy. When I was like 19 I was drunk. It wasn't that good, and he tried to feel me up, but my brother showed up and promptly put a stop to that. It reminded me of a plunger, like he was trying to drag my tongue out of my mouth. It was gross an put me off kissing or boys for a very long time."

I'm glad to hear that someone was on her side even if it was her brother, I would have seen red myself. As an older brother, I know I would happily let the world burn before I ever let it hurt Helen, and I'm glad Konstantin was able to put a stop to any drunken harassment. No one deserves to lose their virginity in a drunken mistake, especially to someone who can't read a woman's body language properly and doesn't understand the word consent. A man who can't kiss well. I mentally shook my head, hoping like hell someone handed that guy his over-entitled ass back to him in a painful way.

"When I was still at university Alexandra played with my breasts," she continues, head dipped low.

Um, excuse me? Alexandra got to touch her? Got to hold her? A zap of jealousy streaked across my mind, that her friend got to touch her soft breasts. How do I get into that kind of friendship? Dude, calm those thoughts right the fuck down now. She's your subject, not your lover.

"She said it was an experiment to find out if I was interested in women, or just a bit of a prude. And turns out it was more of the prude and my sky-high standards than my liking woman. It's not that I haven't been interested in people before, I just..." She stops for a second seeming to need to find the words and sighing deeply.

I had a deep sense of distrust of Alexandra before I learned this titbit, but it's now it's forming into an ever-present dislike of the woman. And not just because she felt Misha up despite her likely being uncomfortable with the situation. Sasha seems to be incredibly manipulative, which based on the research Simon sent on her, really doesn't surprise me, especially considering her upbringing as the only daughter of a Russian oligarch, essentially a spoilt princess.

"I'm just so used to the teasing and people only wanting me because I'm something different. Someone dating me could have been teased for having a 'mail order girlfriend' and I can't stand the idea of that..." She continues, letting loose all of her insecurities. I can't help but appreciate this woman for being brave enough to tell me all of this. Seeing her being trusting enough to be this vulnerable around me is admirable. She knows it's my literal job to watch her, but showing this kind of trust to know I'm also protecting her in a sense makes my heart feel something warm it hasn't felt since before Dad died.

Also showing that she cares enough for others to not be "saddled' with her in case they get mocked, also shows her selflessness, and makes her career of choice make much more sense to me.

"Sasha took me to a sex shop and told me I wasn't allowed to leave without something. So I've explored myself a little. But ah..." She said with a grimace, "I've never asked for assistance." My ears perk up at that, so she's not a complete newbie at this then. She sniffles, and I can feel the shame radiating off her. She feels safe but is seemingly embarrassed by this. It's nothing to be ashamed of, and I don't think anyone has ever taken the time to be gentle with her, listen to her like this and let her know that.

She starts to curl up on herself and cries softly, and without thinking I curl her up on her side, and I big spoon her, trying to provide some comfort. She cries softly in my arms, and I have to wonder if this is something she's had before, physical comfort from someone outside her family.

"You probably think I'm p-p-pathetic, but I just want to be loved for the right reasons. No one has shown any kind of interest in me outside my Russian heritage." She says still sobbing.

It takes a while, but she cries herself to sleep and I'm stuck here thinking about everything she's overcome to get where she is in complete awe. I mean, not discounting my own struggles, but I never got judged in the same way. If anything after my Dad died girls kept calling and wanting to get together so they could 'fix' my grief. I'm pretty sure I had a chronic case of whiskey dick for at least six of those months until girls really got that I hit then quit it when it comes to women, especially women who want to change me. I couldn't say for sure that was the case though. Those six-ish months are very fuzzy.

I lifted my head to admire her sleeping form, her brows drawn together, and the wild waves of her chestnut hair covering the pillow behind her head. I try to move my arm out from under hers, so I could maybe go and pace, figure out how I can build some rules around her for this intimacy thing, but she grabs onto my forearm tighter murmuring something in Russian under her voice. Her murmurs were light, almost lilting, and it was the sound of a beautiful woman's breathing in my arms and soft, almost musical, murmurs in a foreign language that lulled me into a deep sleep.

I woke with a start, feeling more rested than I had in a long while, perhaps since before I started training in the army. Misha is still softly breathe heavily in my arms, with her relaxed body curled tightly against mine...

Christ! I start internally freaking out.

I can't move. I should move. I need to move, but.

Oh fuck.

My morning hard-on was trying its damnedest to escape my boxers and burrow itself between her legs through the undoubtedly soft cotton sleep shorts she'd been wearing. I don't blame him. Misha is without a doubt the most beautiful woman I've had the pleasure of waking up next to. Not my dicks fault that he recognises that too.

Panicking I know that I can't let her wake up with this between her legs. I can't possibly ruin the trust she's given me by letting her wake up with my hard cock digging in between her thighs.

Cursing I tried to think of everything that might soften it, including things like my brother's horror stories from his deployment, until she softly groaned and rubbed herself up against it.

She's asleep. She can't possibly know what she's doing to me right? Unless this is her body reacting to what it's feeling…

Fuck. I can't be a gentleman if she keeps this up.

I mean, normally I'm attracted to her as well, but in this position, it would be so easy to wake her with pleasurable moans and make her feel better than she ever has before…

Rather than softening, I can feel my dick getting impossibly harder and getting incredibly impatient for a release.

Nope.

I can't think like this. She's the subject of an investigation. Not a lover.

I'd like her to be my lover…

I need to get up, so this situation can go back to being PG rather than something out of a wet dream.

I quietly extracted myself from the bed, gently moving her head from my bicep onto a soft pillow, and leg from between my own. I was being especially careful not to jostle her, thanking the times I've had to practice this move after bad choices and regrettable one-night stands during the whiskey-infused years.

I softly closed the door to the bedroom and sprinted across the apartment to dive into a much-needed cold shower. Knowing that thoughts of Misha's soft curves pressed up next to my hard cock weren't likely to fade from my mind any time soon but knowing how she's felt about the way men have treated her in the past, I knew I had to be respectful and follow her lead when it came to anything intimate. I need it to be her move.

Despite my dicks well thought out, almost painful argument against that.

Chapter Fifteen – Misha

The drive to the airport was frosty. We were on good enough terms and we had tried to do the affection thing a bit but I found I was still very much angry with him about just leaving me like he did a few nights ago.

I mean how dare he. The last few nights we've tried being more affectionate with each other, though working through my awkwardness, and feeling of being unwanted was something I couldn't quite shake.

Checking in at the airport was simple enough, and there was thankfully coffee in the international section of the airport. We both sipped our coffees in silence waiting for the boarding call for our first flight of the two.

Getting onto an aeroplane from Kingsford Smith Airport bound for Dubai International was a daunting thought. It wasn't so much the insane time I was about to spend on an aeroplane, but who I was sitting beside for the whole trip. All 23 hours including a layover.

I tried to push through, we had kissed again since and felt each other's chests, my goodness the man was fit. Though there was nothing quite like the groan he released the first time he got his hands on my breasts, and gently applied pressure to my sensitive nipples. That's as far as we went, though I suspect he's had to self-pleasure in the shower alone to get a release, I think this would have driven any other man completely mad.

He will be my undoing.

Plain and simple.

If I could trust him.

After the night I cried myself to sleep and woke up warm and comfortable in his arms, only for him to extricate himself from the situation and leave, I have struggled to fully accept him. We've not talked about that since but have gotten used to each other's company in close proximity, which is a good thing as we're going to be very close for the next 14 and half hours on the first flight, and even closer for the second flight. Five and a half in the economy section from Dubai to Moscow.

The upside was because the ASIS was paying for Matt's ticket they sprung to get us in Premium economy for the longest leg of the journey, this flight, and the Dubai to Sydney flight back. This is good as Matt really needs the extra leg space, his 6'2" frame wasn't going to be comfortable on an airplane for any extended stretch but this was better than having no space. The upgrade also meant the both of us sat next to each other for the flight, with Matt on the window side. There was no argument about who had the window seat. 14 hours was a long time to be trapped next to someone you've been avoiding. As much as one can when they're literally tasked with watching you.

The flight departed slightly late, though still too early in the morning for my under-caffeinated brain, and we were on our way over to Russia, to go and see the matriarch of my family.

Once we were above the ocean, no longer over Australia, Matt shifted in his seat and turned to face me.

I was watching some trashy reality TV show on the aeroplane screen but not really paying attention, due to the stupidly early start this morning, and how one coffee was not enough to kick-start my brain. I wasn't much in a people mood, more accurately I was in an incredibly sour mood.

"Are you okay?" He asks, concern plain on his face, brows drawn together and for a second, I feel like maybe he cares.

"Yeah. I just always get restless on these long flights." I sigh and try to relax back into my seat. Try being the main word here. Being close to Matt without noticing him is difficult, not just because he's a big man and takes up physical space. But also because of his don't-fuck-with-me aura. And in my case, also being undeniably attracted to him, doesn't help my situation. I can't do anything about it though, not just because we're 40,000 ft above an ocean. But because it would affect his career prospects, as well as mine. I'm trying my damnedest to ignore this feeling.

"So, now I have your undivided attention shall we have a chat about what our plan is when we get there?" He asks, making it fairly obvious that he knows I've been avoiding him a bit while we've prepared for this trip.

"After that night last week you've been distant Misha," he starts.

I slap a hand over his mouth shushing him.

"And why do you think that is Motya? Does the feeling of being unwanted tend to have girls flock to you more?" I seethe.

He sits back and straightens his back at that, a shocked look on his face. Mouth agape, eyes wide, eyebrows nearly reaching his hairline.

"Unwanted?" He asked his face transforming from shocked to confused. "What gave you that impression?"

I sigh, "You slinking out of the bed like I was on a one-night stand perhaps? Only without the sleeping with me part I guess, like I meant nothing to you."

Realisation dawns across his face and he has the audacity to look hurt.

"You don't actually think that do you? I left the bed to be a gentleman. I didn't think you'd want to wake up with my hard dick cushioned up against your arse. I left the bed, so I didn't push past your boundaries. I didn't want him," he says gesturing towards his groin, "to make you feel uncomfortable."

I blushed deeply then, I hadn't realised what I was feeling that morning. I felt comfort, love and safe being held in his big arms pressed against his hard body, obviously with one part of it harder than I realised. I turn my face away from his then, with all parts of me heating from embarrassment.

He grabbed my chin, and gently guided it so I faced him again.

"No. Do not think like that Misha. It wasn't your fault that my body reacted the way it did. Well, I mean, it was a little, but in a positive way. Men tend to have a surge of testosterone in the morning that causes what you may have felt. I just didn't want you to feel like you had to do anything about it or freak out when you felt it, because my dick was trying hard to make himself known. I didn't want to damn us both." He finishes, a light pink flush coving his tanned cheeks.

"We don't have to do anything physical outside of cuddling, and hand-holding like your Babushka might expect of an engaged couple. I am fully capable of keeping my urges to myself."

He releases my chin and shuffles in his seat obviously trying to get more comfortable.

"I'd like that Matt. Can I call you Motya while we're in Russia? Or do you want a pet name?"

He looks at me thoughtfully, considering the request then surprises me.

"I don't really know much about Russian culture. Do people call each other babe? Or is the shortened version of their name what people call each other affectionate at all?"

"People call each other things like kitten or sun. My surname means hare, so my grandmother calls me a little rabbit, Zaychik. I think you suit Luchik. It means sunray, do you mind if I call you that? For me the feminine version of that is Solnishko, or darling is Zótotse."

"I don't mind Luchik, or Motya. Whatever you prefer. If you're speaking, I'll make sure I can respond. Zótotse feels more natural to me, I mean for me to call you if you don't mind. I've just heard that this whole nickname thing is culturally important over there and I just want to make sure I can play the part properly." He starts to get flustered by this and I drop the conversation.

"All right Luchik, we have a solid eight hours left on this flight, shall we just lean up against each other and rest? It will be full on once we get to Moscow, and we will need to be on our game when we're there." I lift the armrest and lean against him. He lifts his arm up so, even in this confined space I can curl up next to him and close my eyes.

"Zótotse," he whispers into my hair.

"Never feel unwanted by me, I struggle to stay professional around you. I want you, I do, but on your terms, and not when I'm working."

I fall asleep then, unable to hear if he whispers any other words in my hair, and hoping he'll still be there when we wake.

Chapter Sixteen- Matt

I woke up to the feeling of a soft body tucked against my side under one of my arms, and a popping sensation in my ears. I knew the time zone changes would mess with my sleeping patterns but being honest I hadn't slept all that much since the morning I left Misha in my bed alone. I still feel bad about how she perceived that move, but I thought at the time I was doing the right thing.

Our flight was descending into Dubai, and we had about four hours to kill before our connecting flight to Moscow.

"Is there anything you want to do while we wait for our next flight?" I ask Misha, waking her up from her light slumber against my chest. Her big chocolate eyes stared up at me sleepily through her thick lashes and I could feel my heart melting. I quietly curse John again for setting me on this assignment, hating that I have to remain professional around her.

"We can't be affectionate while in Dubai though, and you'll want a scarf to cover this," I say curling one of her waves around my finger. This act of affection made her sigh in contentment and cuddle closer, something I wasn't sure was possible.

"Sleepy Zótotse, you've got to wake up and put your seatbelt back on properly. We're only 10 minutes away from landing." That caught her attention, and she snapped her eyes open, she sat up, and moved back into her assigned seat rather than half of mine. I found I missed her warmth pressed against my right side but knew that I needed to snap out of this feeling of strong fondness for her. I'm meant to only be acting, it's not meant to be the real thing. My job and hers were on the line.

"I usually eat my way through the airport, or if I haven't slept on the flight, I'll go grab one of those fancy sleep pod things,"

Misha says starting to straighten herself out and stretching her arms up towards the roof of the plane.

Food, that's something I can do. Sleep, probably not at this point, but I can always browse the stores, and who knows maybe a book will capture my attention.

"Okay we shall eat our way through Dubai International Airport, and your Babushka will have to get someone to roll us out of the connecting flight," I say looking over to her.

She giggled at that, which caused something to happen in my chest, a warmth or a fluttering or something. I should probably book in with my doctor when I get back from this trip, just to double check there is nothing wrong with my heart.

We settled into a McDonald's meal as we waited for our connecting flight to Moscow.

We sat down in the food court and I started picking at my fries.

"Wanna play a game?" Misha asks me as I am lifting a burger to my mouth.

I take a bite and with a crooked eyebrow nod.

"Okay, this was something my Mama used to do with Kostya and me when we travelled for a long time," She started to explain.

"So pick a person, and maybe we start properly once we've had our food. But we choose a person, and we guess why they're at the airport and the best story wins."

I look at her sceptically, mouth still full of burger and eyebrow still raised.

"Point at someone, and I'll start then?" she says and I point at a woman sitting at a café not too far from us.

Her hair is up in a long dark ponytail with a silk scarf tied into it, she's wearing relaxed jeans, a t-shirt and sneakers. She lifts her sunglasses up as she looks down at her phone and brings her coffee up to her lips to take a sip. Her eyes close as the coffee must hit her taste buds, and perhaps it was that part of her behaviour I clung to when Misha started weaving a story for me.

"She's an international traveller from a country with good coffee, maybe New Zealand or Australia. She's tripping to somewhere in Europe and isn't staying long, as you can see she has a ponytail, and while she could use the scarf in her hair to cover her hair, perhaps she did that when she got off the flight here.

Just in case she needed to. That also says to me she's an unsure traveller, perhaps why that coffee is hitting her now. She didn't get any before her previous flight, because she was so ready to get on the plane to get to her destination. She's wearing sneakers, but they're a good brand so she's not lacking funds, her jeans look new, and the T-shirt is from a concert that came through a few months ago in Australia.

Yeah, I reckon she was on the same flight as us. My guess on where she's going... Maybe England, so setting up shop in England. With her relaxed fit, perhaps she's a nurse or maybe she's going into nannying? So yeah. That's what I think."

I look at her then, and back at the woman in question who grabs a small carry-on suitcase from next to her and hurries away towards an international gate.

A burst of static comes over the loudspeaker and an announcement starts, "We are calling all passengers on flight BAW106 to please make their way to the gate printed on their ticket as we will be starting the boarding process shortly. Thank you."

The next flight was likely to be less comfortable, five hours stuck in economy with less foot room. But being in a good spot with Misha meant that the flight would be pretty bearable in comparison to being next to a stranger on the very full and cramped plane.

We were squashed up together on this flight. I understood why some people called this cattle class. As awkward as this would be with a stranger, with Misha it felt comfortable.

I let her snuggle in tightly into my left side as I kept a straight spine in the middle seat of the row. I wish I had managed to convince my boss to pay for the emergency exit at least, but I knew after paying for the upgrade for Misha, and my flights to and from Moscow, putting more strain on the Australian taxpayer wouldn't go down well. My knees were likely to cramp after a few hours, and getting up would probably be a taxing effort.

"It's magical," she says wistfully.

"Moscow that is, the buildings look like they're from a fairy-tale. The history is so exceptionally rich. The food is incredible." She sighs thinking about all the undoubtedly very great food she's planning on indulging while we're over here.

"Yeah?" I ask, "Tell me about it?"

"Well, the Silk Road came through Russia. And we had the Tzars. And while that didn't end in the best way, one of my favourite fairy tales was always The Tale of the Dead Tsarevna and the Seven Bogatyrs. Kind of like Snow white that we have in English, but with a Russian Orthodox twist.

We don't really have much in the way of WW1 history sites, but plenty of WW2-affected cities, and the history of the battles there is really interesting.

The night scene in Moscow can't be beaten, and Piter has the most incredible live music scene.

The food is just..." she trails off wistfully. Getting lists of menus sorted in her mind and scheming on taking me to all sorts of restaurants I'm sure.

Due to flight delays, we landed in Moscow six and a half hours later. Misha had managed to call her grandmother to let her know we were running late and were going to be fighting against rush hour traffic heading to our destination.

I hope Misha booked a hotel, as that would give us a bit of reprieve from each other while I'm still able to keep an eye on anything suspicious.

We board the train from the airport and head into the city centre, into the bear's den.

Chapter Seventeen - Misha

The hustle and bustle of Russian public transport reminds me fondly of summers when Mama flew Kostya and me over to Moscow and we had to get our way to Babushkas.

The sound of Russian being spoken loudly around us was probably overwhelming for Motya but gave me an incredible sense of homecoming.

I'd only really spent a short amount of time in Russia since the big move to Australia. The longest trip was funded by Sasha's dad who wanted her back in Russia during the Winter Olympics. Not that we spent much time in Sochi, but we got to travel most of the country during that time and Sasha got to see it like a tourist for the first time.

We visited Vladik again, over the frozen lands of Serbia, down towards the Caspian Sea and over to the most 'European' part of Russia in Kaliningrad. We spent the five days on the train gossiping about university friends and talking about our plans for the future.

We danced in the streets with others as clubs closed for the night in Moscow.

We drank vodka with young men who were perusing Sasha in St Petersburg, well we were, before her father's men scared them off.

We drank in the history, and the culture and it made me fall in love with some of the history, though I had strong opinions about the political landscape that currently ruled over Russia.

The sights, sounds and smells remind me of this beautiful country. But if you haven't visited before and have the distinct disadvantage of not speaking the language, the vastness might be a little intimidating.

Just as we get off the flight, Matt asks me to explain to him what he can expect, while we wait for our luggage to arrive on the belt.

"Will it be cold? What can I expect?"

"I mean, it'll be chillier than Sydney, but it's March, so it is getting warmer here. Uh. I think people are a little like Sydney folk. In the sense that most people just want to get on with it. I mean Moscow is like that. It can be a bit different in different cities. Like St Petersburg is full of beautiful art history, so is Volgograd, but for World War Two history. There are some roads out east that were built by prisoners of war that if you're keen we could check out. Um, Moscow has an awesome music scene..." I'm interrupted by someone bumping into me.

Hard.

"Mne zhal'!" a deep voice says.

"Maxim Komarov?" I asked the male figure who was hurrying away into the crowd of people rushing to get home after work.

He stops in his tracks. "Misha?" he asks in a thick Russian accent, as he turns around.

Maxim, or Max, is Sasha's younger brother and someone who is incredibly sheltered in his family. Seeing him now as a grown man was a little startling.

Sasha doesn't talk about him much, he is very much her father's favourite and the Medvezhonok of the family, something she is a bit sour about.

"How are you?" I ask him as he turns to face me, "It's been what, like five years? How are your family?"

He smiles, in a way I'm sure has melted more than a few girl's hearts in the past few years since I was last over this side of the world. He really has come into his early 20s.

"Misha, please excuse my impoliteness," he addresses me in flawless English because of course, he would.

"I can see your male counterpart and yourself have had a long journey, one assumes from Australia? And I myself am in a bit of a hurry to get back to Piter. I hope you can understand and not consider this a slight against me or my family." He finishes with a nod.

"Oh of course," I say reaching out for a hand shake. He grabs my hand in a very firm grip and shakes it twice before letting go.

"Tell my sister to visit da? Her mat' misses her." He says and within seconds is swallowed up in the crowd.

I turn to face Matt and shrug. Perhaps that was a good example of what people are like around here more often than not.

We got out of the train in the middle of the city. I know Babushka is expecting us but I am also acutely aware that this is Matt's first time in Russia and I want to introduce him in the best way possible, by showing him some of the best sights to be seen in the central city, and visiting some of my favourite restaurants while we're here. The train was predictably busy, it is the busiest public transport network in the world and proudly so, and I know I was glad to be out of the cramped cabin when we got into the city centre.

"We're here!" I declare to Matt in English and drag him out of the train cabin onto the street, taking in the air and revelling in the fact I'm soon to see one of my favourite humans.

"What do you want to see while you're here?" I ask turning to him.

He looked a little shell-shocked. Winter in Moscow is mild compared to Vladivostok but it was drizzly and grey today, perhaps a tad off-putting for a boy from Sunny Sydney. His eyes were wild as he took in the sites, and I started dragging him towards Red Square.

"Um, I'm not sure. I guess seeing the famous cathedrals would be cool. But I'm working on this trip Misha, I mean Zótotse. What's good?" He said shrugging and following me around.

I squeak with excitement, "Oh we have to go to a few of my favourite restaurants and of course St Basils Cathedral. I need to show you some of the most beautiful spots this city has to offer, and some of the best food you'll ever have the pleasure to eat." I say getting more enthusiastic as we go on.

The walk to the square doesn't take long, and as we get there I can feel Matt tense up next to me.

I look up to him, the question of what was wrong on my tongue before he pulls us back and away from the square.

"Why did you bring me here?" he hissed. I looked at him, confusion was evident on my face as I could feel my eyes widen and brows draw together.

"What do you mean Luchik?" I asked as he wasn't taking the visual confusion on my face as a cue to tell me what was wrong.

A few passersby looked at us and I waved them off, explaining in sharp Russian that it was a lovers quarrel and none of their business.

"Really Mikhaila? The damned Kremlin? You're accused of being a spy, and the first place you bring your foreign minder is the Government buildings? It doesn't look good," he hisses at me.

Realisation dawned on my face, and I could feel my jaw drop in horror at his accusation.

"No Matthew, that wasn't... Let's go to a café, and I'll explain." I say taking him away from the square, and towards a café on one of the off-streets.

We sit at a table towards the back of the café and he orders a coffee, and I order myself a tea.

"Luchik, let me explain." I was interrupted by the server "Spasibo," I say to her and she disappears away to leave us to it.

"Alright Mikhaila, explain. And I hope it's good. Because I'm a bit freaked out at the moment, and I am not in the mood for political talking around or lies." Matthew says looking over the lip of his coffee cup, taking a sip.

"Spasibo Luchik. How much do you know about Russian history? About what are considered the tourist attractions in Moscow?" I look at him over my tea, and he shrugs, so I continue.

"I wasn't about to deliver you to the Kremlin. The Kremlin is just a fortified building. Think like a British castle. Yes, there are government buildings within its walls but that's not all. And they aren't likely to be watching or guarding the outer walls. There are guided tours around some of the buildings in the square because it's so rich with history. It's typically the first-place people want to see when they visit Moscow, and I didn't think you would be an exception to that rule. I wanted to show you St Basils, and then we could have had a peek at the likes of the historic armoury. Perhaps not today, we can come up with a list at Babushkas this evening and go from there."

"Wait. Your grandmothers, this evening?" He asked, looking a bit taken aback.

"Da Motya, Where do you think we would be staying?"

He blanches at that, and I was a little worried by his reaction.

"I thought you might have had a hotel or something. Perhaps nearby, but not staying with your elderly grandmother." He says, his eyes wide and searching my face for the answer he wants.

"Sorry Luchik, we're saying with Babushka. She has a two-bedroom place and she would be incredibly offended if her Zaychik and her fiancée didn't stay with her. We must stay with her, at least for a few nights. If you really want we can do the trans-Siberian and I can show you Vladivostok, we could go up to St Petersburg. If we go to Vladivostok, we can change our flights from there to go through Singapore home." I explain.

"Come, let's go to Babushka's home, and from here we can plan the rest of the trip. We're over here for three and a half weeks and we should spend at least four nights in Moscow, anything less would upset Babushka."

Chapter Eighteen - Matt

I wasn't sure what the heck I was in for when we arrived in Moscow, but being dragged through a very busy airport, being confronted by a man from Misha's past, into a very busy train then my finding walking through streets was a bit of a reprieve from the busy crowds, until I noticed we were right in front of the Kremlin. The Russian government buildings.

I didn't know the ins and outs of Dad's death, but the IED that exploded the vehicle he was in, and led to his eventual death, was laid by Russian soldiers when they were in Afghanistan, and my job at the moment is as a literal spy. Which was not what I wrote on my migration card.

My vision narrowed and I could feel my heart rate rise like I was under attack, undoubtedly what my brother had felt on the battlefield. My chest tightened and I could feel a lot of my muscles tensing. The hand of Misha's I was holding was tense, and I was focusing on not crushing her knuckles together while I tried to figure out what this feeling was. Blood pounded in my ears, drowning out the sound of the crowd, and the sound of everything else except my shallow breathing.

What is happening to me?

Is this a panic attack?

In one of the worst places for it, right in front of the Government buildings of a hostile government, the embodiment of the enemy in my mind.

In my mind that increased the danger tenfold.

How could Misha be so careless? She couldn't possibly have known about my father, but I still work in the Australian government as a spy, not something I would have thought she would have forgotten easily, as she's the subject of my investigation.

Then she let me know that we're staying with her grandmother who I haven't met. After we ran into a man who she seemed to know well at the airport.

I'm out of my depth, feeling like I was thrown into the deep in without knowing how to swim. Just managing to flail enough to keep my head above water.

As we walk through the streets of Moscow, to get to the tram that goes past our accommodation for the next few nights, I drag my hands down my face.

Okay, Matthew Stephen Taylor. You've survived 8 months of military training, a bout of alcoholism and rehab, ASIS training, and university as a 'mature' student. And now you find yourself in a less than friendly country, not speaking the language and about to meet the only family of the stunning woman you're crushing on but is also your subject to monitor for work and is under investigation for potentially spying on the country your family has given their lives to protect.

The pep talk did nothing to soothe my nerves.

I tried to do research on Russian customs and culture, before coming over here but I don't think I was really all that prepared for the complete difference in sounds and sights. I also should have realised that the square Misha took me to has St Basils Cathedral in it, the damned building I told her I wanted to see.

Instead, I freaked out like a complete idiot, and I've made her feel like shit for doing that.

And because everyone is speaking Russian, I can't even distract myself by listening to conversations, I'm just stuck in my own head as we get off the tram and Misha looks up at me as we stand in front of an apartment block.

"Are you okay Luchik?" She looks at me with worry in her eyes. I am the worst pretend fiancée in history. And it's probably my shitty attitude that's probably causing her to pause.

"Yes, Zótotse, I just. I think I'm overwhelmed."

Okay, so that might be an understatement.

Exhausted from a battle with my own mind perhaps or drained from the potent mixture of anxiety and grief hitting me like a tsunami in a very public space.

"Luchik, we'll rest when we get to Babushka's. We've just done a huge amount of travel, and I get that you're in a foreign country where you don't speak the language. I shouldn't have dropped right into 'host the tourist' mode. I'm sorry," she says dipping her chin in a subconsciously submissive gesture.

Normally I would have corrected her, and the submissiveness of her statement should probably have set off some flags as well, but I really was caught up in my own mind, with the melodic sounds of a foreign language drifting through my ears.

We knock on a painted wooden door. Intricate flowers adorn the lilac background and speaks to the hours of work and care put into this first impression of the Zaitsev home. The number 43 was also painted on the door, in a big bold font. This shows that this apartment has pride of place among other apartments that didn't have as brightly coloured entrances.

An elderly woman, slightly hunched but probably only just over five feet, opens the door. A scarf adorns her grey curled hair, and her blue eyes sparkle with mischief, something that her granddaughter inherited. She's frail and moves slowly, but it's obvious she still has a zest for life in the way that she speaks.

"Vkhodite Pozhaluysta," she says looking at us both as she dips her chin and shuffles back into the house.

"Come in, please," Misha whispers to me in translation as we walk in.

"Babushka's English isn't great, and she will probably speak to me in Russian. I can ask her to try English, but I can also translate for you?" She looks up at me with that, her big milk chocolate eyes pleading for some reason. Perhaps for understanding. As if I would judge an elderly woman's language skills, especially when it's not her first language and he wouldn't likely have been exposed to it throughout her life in Russia.

I pull out my phone and show Misha its new translate live function.

"I'm hoping to be able to use this?" I say looking down at her hopefully, I know the technology for this kind of thing can be hit or miss but hopefully, it'll save me from any potentially awkward situations.

"At least to get the general idea of what is going on. I don't know if I could respond in Russian though, I think if I got the phone to try it might sound super robotic, so you may need to help me there," I say pointing down at my phone, already trying to translate the conversation back into Russian.

"Okay, if you're sure Motya." She gives my bicep a gentle squeeze, probably to wish me good luck but the whole day has frankly gone to shit, so I'm not sure how much worse it can get. If it can get worse...

After a quiet dinner of classic Russian food and delectable desserts, with Misha's grandmother trying to speak in broken English to me, and me speaking in English probably too quickly back to her, trying to slow it right down and attempting to speak without my Australian accent and also trying to pick up the occasional Russian word to pepper into conversation with her.

"Done?" She asks as she starts to clear the plates off the table.

"The food was wonderful, Spasibo," I say nodding at her and using one of the words I'd learned in the past few days, thank you.

I glanced around the room and noticed, that Anna, the first name of Misha's Babushka, only had three lounge chairs, all mismatches, and undoubted second hand, but no couch. It made me wonder how else the house might be furnished.

"I show you room now?" She asks us both, and Misha nods.

She leads us down a short hallway to the second bedroom of her apartment. I'm momentary in shock because the spare room is identical to the set-up that Misha has in her home back in Sydney.

I look at Misha, and she shrugs with a sheepish smile.

I gulp, and Misha shoots me a look as if to say, 'I know, we will sort it out, but say anything and I'll track down the Bratva and give them your number or give you up to the Russian government.' Okay maybe not that intense, but the love this woman has for her grandmother is immense, so it wouldn't surprise me if she did turn me over to the Russian authorities if I ever did go against Anna.

Yawning, I say "Thank you so much for hosting us, Anna, we've done a lot of travelling and must have an early night's rest. Good night."

"Spokoynoy nochi," Anna says dipping her head in farewell as she shuffles out of the room and closes the door behind her.

I quickly turn to face Misha, fear, and panic probably evident on my face.

There's only one bed.

Chapter Nineteen – Misha

"Spokoynoy nochi," my Babushka says dipping her head in farewell as she slowly shuffles out of the room and closes the door behind her.

Babushka is looking older, a little frailer, a little more like she's more breakable than she's ever seemed. She moves slower, though with determination to be unaided.

It's obvious she's missed me and wanted to see me, but I can't help but worry that this might be the last visit I make to her here in Russia. Not only does it seem to take an age to get here, and there was no way she'd come to Australia, but I honestly wasn't sure how much longer she'd live and what she has to live for.

Living through World War two, the Cold War, and the hard times that came with the Soviet Government, even if our family wasn't too poorly off during these times, will have taken a toll on her. If not her physical health, then on her soul. Add in her husband who towards the end of his life wasn't a very nice man and that would have aged her as well.

A thought that scares me deeply. I know she wants to be with her husband in the afterlife, but surely, she wants to see her grandchildren's milestones first. A wedding, a great-grandchild perhaps. To witness us falling in love.

I worry that we won't have that much more time together before she passes away to be with her husband. A thought I dread. Dedushka wasn't a nice man, and all I want in this world is to have more time with my Babushka. Her hugs are the best, her cooking is only bested by Kostya, and the world would be quieter without her laugh echoing through her apartment, and more often than not, down the phone line to me.

I'm deep in that thought when Matt whirls around to face me, sheer panic marring his beautiful face, catching me off guard, enough to need to stifle a giggle. His eyes were wide, brows pinched together and lips in a tight line.

"Come on Motya, it's not that bad," I say trying to placate him out of his current alarmed state.

My words cause a glare, and he starts towards me causing me to back up and pinning me back against the closed bedroom door.

When his hands reach my shoulders, he brings his lips down to hover above my pulse. I instinctively tilt my head to the side to give him better access.

As if I wanted him to kiss me there. Do I want him to kiss me? Do I want to kiss him?

His lips brush over the spot and he whispers quietly in my ear.

"Misha, I'm working while we're here, and we can't afford the distraction..." I reach behind him to his back and pull him flush to me like a hug, my breasts pressed into his chest.

I think I do want his kisses, even if I'm not sure entirely what it means. His breath quickens and he moans as he kisses my neck, causing his growing erection to press against my soft belly and my nipples to tighten into stiff peaks in response to feeling him get excited for me.

I gasp at the realisation of the effect I've had on him, but he keeps kissing around my neck and ear, and it just...

Feels. So. Damned. Good.

My breathing quickens, and I pull his head back gently by his hair and look into his eyes. His pupils were blown so there was only a thin ring of his striking deep green irises, highlighting my own sense of want as I realised I could very easily get lost in this man. He would be my ruin.

Big mistake but stay strong Misha. He's just a man. You've been around men before. Do not let your hor...

I moan as he starts caressing my collarbone and down my chest to tease my hypersensitive nipples under my bra.

"Motya," I whimper, "We can't," I say shutting my eyes because the removal of his hands and closeness would be physically painful at the moment. And I don't want to see it coming if it comes to that.

His head drops to my shoulder, and he lets out a long-pained breath.

"It's a bad idea, Matt, my Babushka is old but not deaf." I regret the words as they leave my mouth, not in a disrespectful manner, particularly regarding my grandmother, but I needed this man like I needed oxygen.

He backs up a bit and groans, "This is why a hotel would have been a better idea."

"She thinks we're engaged, to be married; she expects that we're quite likely sleeping next to each other but saving ourselves until our wedding day. Its tradition. That I'm still a…" I drift off then and can feel myself shrinking into myself a little. I hate that I still feel a slight sense of shame about my virginity.

He grabs my chin and tilts my face up towards his.

"Misha, do not be ashamed of that. It's not a turn-off and nothing to be ashamed of. Can you tell just how much I want you?" He says, gaze tilting towards the obvious outline of his cock in his pants.

"If you want me in that way, if you want to test the waters and see where this leads then you need to trust me. We can take it as slow as you want. But we can't do this while I'm at the ASIS. When we get back to Sydney, I'll report my findings and get off this case and we can look into what we are then?" He looks up at me hopefully, eyes still blown with lust, but there is a pleading in there.

I know better than to expect anything, but I couldn't help a glimmer of hope, to finally feel what Sasha gushes about when she's dating someone, a love like my parents. Something I honestly didn't think I wanted. But I want it with him.

"We should have gotten a hotel," he murmurs under his breath and stepping back from me, going towards the back of the room.

Getting space from me so he doesn't act on his earlier feelings. Especially as the bulge in his pants isn't getting any smaller. In fact, it seems to be getting larger.

Which, fuck. If we ever do end up... how will it fit?

His comment shouldn't hurt, but it does, a little. I don't think he realises how much work goes into hosting someone, or what the culture expects of us in Russia.

Undoubtedly Babushka spent days cleaning until the house was spotless, She didn't need to but it is part of being Russian. We must have a spotless home when people come to visit, especially people who haven't visited before. It's a first impression thing, but more than that. It's almost at the point of national pride.

I step forward from the door, feeling less crowded now Matt has backed off, "Babushka hired someone to come and clean before we got here. It would be insulting to leave without being here for a few nights. After that, we can travel around a bit and see Russia outside of Moscow. Depending on what you want to see, we can change our outgoing flights or connect them from another city."

We both walk over to the bed then, a little unsure of what to do in this situation.

"I can change into Pyjamas, and we go to sleep clothed, yes?" I ask looking over at him.

He nods, "Are there other cushions or blankets or something? We could make a wall between us."

Little did he know, after some of his reactions, one was already being built in my mind, I couldn't afford to be hurt by someone who would just use me.

Chapter Twenty – Matt

We built a blanket wall between us to sleep that night, which got thrown aside during the night, both of us sleeping fitfully. I woke up with my cock hard as a rock, and with a stunningly beautiful woman wrapped up in my arms as a little spoon.

Years of living in a military family meant I was a naturally early riser. This means because I woke before her and noticed my body's reaction, I tried to extract myself from her grip around my arms and re-erect the blanket wall. I topped it off by putting a pillow around the groin area so she wouldn't freak out waking up to my hard dick trying to bury itself between her legs, not that a pillow does much good in hiding it.

Even the thought of that had me groaning so I rolled over in the bed, only to find her cuddling up to me like a koala and I'm her favourite eucalyptus tree, soft and warm against my back.

"Hey, are you okay?" she asks her voice thick with sleep.

"Da Misha," I respond quickly in the little Russian I've picked up in the last few months.

She moans and I turn my head to look at her, also praying for my cock to go down. Because that moan really didn't help it go away.

"Are you okay?" I ask her, as that moan could only be one of two things, either she's turned on, or she's hurt. I prefer the former but I'm not ready to make assumptions.

She wakes up a little more with that question. "Yeah," she says yawning and shuffling herself back onto her side of the bed detaching herself from my back.

"What's the plan today?" I ask, turning back around, and with the space she's left, I feel like I can breathe again, and there's a twinge of sadness when I realise her moving away means I can't smell her hair in the same way.

She turns to look at me, looking pointedly in the eye. "I don't know. Will you freak out on me today? Should we try and plan the rest of the trip out a little?"

She's mad. Why is she so mad?

I guess I should have picked up on the little cues. On how when she was sleepy, just before she woke up she wanted to press herself closer to me and my body, but as soon as she was awake enough to speak she shuffled away.

She had been mad, in a quiet seething kind of way, on the flights over. I mean I knew I had probably done something. Or at least that's what Helen would tell me.

Christ, what I would do for a 10-minute phone call with her to try and figure this shit out.

Was it something to do with last night? She understood that I couldn't do anything until I've resigned from the ASIS or at the very least renounced my involvement in this case.

Misha is now sitting up in the bed, glaring daggers my way when she doesn't think I notice. Her arms are crossed across her chest pressing down her breasts, which is something I really shouldn't be focusing on right now.

"Um yeah, probably a good idea to consider some other parts of this country to visit. I don't want to be offensive to your granny or anything, but I've not come to Russia before. I think I should see some of it, it's not like I'm likely to ever end up coming back. But first, can I ask because I'm not sure why..." I drift off. She quirks an eyebrow at me, and I'm forced to continue awkwardly.

Fuck.

My sister Helen would have my balls for even considering asking this. Likely complaining that I never listened to her when she tried to give me advice about girls.

"Why are you mad at me?" I cringe internally. I know that's the last thing you ask a girl, but I really cannot figure out what I did that was so bad.

"Really Matt? Where are your detective skills? Isn't observation a critical element of becoming a fucking spy?" I visibly cringe and send her some puppy dog eyes.

I'm under-caffeinated, and I just woke up. But she's right. I need to pay more attention.

"You freak out in the Red Square then stay silent. The way you look at me and react to me like you want me, but your words say the opposite. It seems like all you want to do is get out of here. Like my family's presence offends you, and I'm sick of the constant fucking silence." She says arms flying up, her shirt lifting slightly and giving me a peek at her soft belly.

"You need to tell me what the hell is going on, or maybe I'll see about getting you sent back to Australia, and I'll just stay here." She crosses her arms again across her chest with that, pressing her breasts together making them look fucking fantastic.

Fuck. Matt.

Head out of the gutter!

Focus.

"Um. All right, Misha, that's a lot, and I'm so sorry that I'm not expressing what I'm feeling because it's a lot for me. I'm so sorry. I can talk about everything, but I need to be in a safe place to do so. Have you got anywhere where we can be anonymous? Also, a few things I'll say may be politically sensitive, and the last thing I want to do while I'm overseas, is piss off the government. Do you know a place I can talk openly?"

She sighs, "I can ask Babushka if she knows anywhere, We could just talk in here. Or ask her to visit one of the other grandmothers in the block?"

I nod at that, but just as Misha gets up "We would need to do a bug sweep before I talk too. I know it's a bit invasive, but I prefer to be safe rather than sorry with this."

She raises an eyebrow but leaves the room. Hips swaying and slamming the door shut as she goes.

I'm in trouble here. A lot more than I think either of us realise.

She comes back twenty minutes later.

"Babushka has gone to play Durak with one of her neighbours. The woman is highly competitive, so I think we've bought ourselves a couple of hours. What do we do about the bug search? How can I help?"

We do a sweep of the living room and a more in-depth search of the bedrooms. Lifting couch cushions, checking under the table and chairs, in the lamp shades. Matt lifted up the beds and mattresses and stuck his ear in the cupboard so he could listen for the slight buzz that one of these devices can often give off.

Nothing was found, which I expected, but you can never be too careful.

"Tea?" Misha asks pulling out the tools to make traditional Russian tea, as I've learned in the last couple of days.

"Um, sure. Black with one sugar, not jam. I've seen what you do to make tea sweet." I fake a shudder and I'm treated to a small smile cracking Misha's toughened exterior.

She makes the tea and I start explaining myself.

"My father died in 2012, about five months after a Russian IED blew apart most of his convoy. He died from the injuries after six months of agony in an Australian hospital.

I'm part of a military family, my brother is currently serving in the Middle East, and I was meant to... Well, I guess you've noticed

I don't drink. My dad's death sent me into a bit of a tailspin. I got hooked on the escape that alcohol provides.

It ruined all my progress with the army, as I had enrolled and was over halfway through my first year of training. I was discharged. Not dishonourably thankfully, but not with recommendations either. I ended up in a local rehabilitation centre. It meant I couldn't drink, because once I started I physically couldn't stop and I had too many hospital visits to pump my stomach in 2013 and 2014. The damage done to my liver from it is probably chronic and well, I can heal a little by not touching booze, I guess?

I'll just live a shorter life than the average person...

That was why I freaked out when we were in the Red Square. I saw the Kremlin, which frankly has been a scapegoat for a lot of the blame I have for my own failings, and my father's death, and the desire to drink came back tenfold, and I just...

I needed to get the hell out of there. I needed out before I threw away my sobriety and asked to go to a bar. It really doesn't help the way I've chosen to serve Australia, as an intelligence agent," I say with my hand sweeping my hair back. It's gotten longer.

I look over to where Misha is perched on her seat, staring up at me through her thick lashes, with her chocolate brown eyes starting to water.

"I had no idea, Matt," she starts but I put my hand up to stop her, I'm not here for her sympathy.

"I'm not here for pity or sorrow or whatever. I am giving an explanation as to why I freaked out and reacted the way I did. It'll give some insight into what I can and cannot handle in this country. Also, I guess it explains my sobriety." I say, making sure that I'm being clear with my situation with a shrug.

"Okay, with that in mind, is there anything in particular you want to do while we're here in Russia?" she asks, changing the subject.

"Um, perhaps some of the military history? I want to see not just the pretty history. I want to see the real Russia, and not shy away from the hard stuff. I can take a photo with you at St Basil's, but I'm going to need some advance notice so I can mentally prepare myself, to even go near any government buildings. Does that give you some ideas to work with?"

She nods, "Grab a book Luchik, I'll start planning. I'll go grab Babushka though, she has seen a lot of Russia in her time and should have some good ideas." She bounds away excited that the holiday is back on.

I'm just here hoping that I haven't set myself up for failure in being around her in close proximity for the next few weeks. Either to push her boundaries or that she might drive me to drink.

Chapter Twenty-One – Misha

Matt is on the couch with a book and I'm furiously typing away at my laptop, shouting ideas in Russian at Babushka who is in the kitchen making dinner.

"Matt, do the Tzars and that kind of military history interest you at all?"

He looks up and nods at me.

"Good! I think I have it!" I shout as I bound over to Matt shoving a handwritten note under his nose.

Four nights - Moscow. Explore the history and enjoy the river. Mandatory stay with Babushka.

Two nights - St Petersburg. Fly to Pieter from Moscow to save time. Enjoy the architecture, visit the museum, and see the church of the Saviour on spilled blood.

Two nights in Yekaterinburg - Catch a red-eye flight to the city and visit the church on the blood. Learn about the history and get a sense of the 'real' Russia.

Two nights Kazan. Take the train from Yekaterinburg to Kazan and visit its Mosque. Enjoy more local cuisine (ideally without drooling, which may be hard)

Two nights in Volgograd - visit the motherland called Statue and visit the war museum that highlights the battle of Stalingrad.

Three nights Kaliningrad. Beachside city to get a very different taste of Russia. Fly back from Kaliningrad to connect to our flights leaving Moscow.

"How does that sound?" I ask peering down at him reading my note.

I know this is totally giving off golden retriever energy but fuck it. I'm excited to travel with him and make him happy.

Wait.

When did those feelings start?

"It feels like a lot, how are we travelling most of the time? I'm not comfortable driving on the right side of the road." He says looking at me sceptically.

This has the effect of managing to break me out of a spiral of overthinking and analysing every conversation I've had with Matt.

Shaking my head slightly I say "The train is pretty good in most of the country, but I can drive on the right side. I may have learnt how to drive here, rather than in Sydney. Blame Babushka."

I laugh, feeling a little self-conscious about it. Most kids learned to drive with their parents, but in the Australian summer school holidays I often came back to Russia. While it was winter over here, Babushka taught me to drive in the old car Dedushka left when he passed away. She didn't mind if it got dinged up or scaped, she just wanted to give me some freedom while I stayed with her, much to the disapproval of my parents.

"What do we want to do today? Should we do the Square? Or maybe we could visit the zoo? They have Pandas." I look over to Matt for approval and he nods.

I get excited and squeal.

"Okay. I'll look up the train timetable, and we'll need to grab proper coffee on the way. That's one thing Australia does better for sure. From memory, there's a Coffee Like around the entrance."

I race off to get ready for Matt's first proper day in Russia.

It was perfect. It felt like a date and the only people we were lying to were ourselves.

I think in my plan I failed to consider how much of a first date-like location the zoo might be. Ice cream, coffee, and cute fluffy animals, it was a beautiful afternoon.

A 21.5-hectare zoo is the largest in Russia, with pandas, polar bears and a myriad of different animals from around the world. Walking around it took quite a few hours, and there's nothing quite like animals to bring out one's inner child.

"What is your favourite animal?" I ask up at Matt as we wander past some incredibly cute sulphur-crested cockatoos. We see them when we leave the city in Australia, but seeing them here, in Russia, brings back a sense of homesickness I wasn't expecting.

"I like ravens." He states simply.

"Ravens?" I ask looking up at him. I mean his hair is dark and he's smart so I guess it fits.

"Yeah. There is a species that's native to Australia, they mate for life. They're super smart and are usually peaceful unless provoked. They're known as tricksters and heroes in Aboriginal culture."

Well, I didn't know that.

"What's yours?" He says, while also pointing towards a bird trying to do something funny.

"Pandas." It's simple. They're cute and can be dumb as hell, which makes for great internet memes.

"Really?"

"Yep, they're cute. And they are a little dumb. Kinda like me sometimes right?" I respond, looking back up at him.

He crooks an eyebrow at that, reserving his judgement on the situation.

We got home a few hours later to Babushkas to find a note in Cyrillic on top of a small pile of 1,000 Ruble notes.

"What does it say?" Matt asks peering over my shoulder in curiosity.

"I went to a game night. Please, here's some money so you two can enjoy a romantic dinner. Seems Babushka has gone out for the night. What are you feeling like for dinner?"

And like that, we're going out on a second date, to a Russian Italian restaurant. We took the train down to the Moskva River and walked riverside before heading up the street towards the restaurant. It was a relaxed atmosphere and we walked into the restaurant holding hands. Again, only lying to ourselves.

After a filling pasta dinner, and a few too many gin brambles on my part, we pay the bill and make our way out of the restaurant.

"So how do we get back to your Nana's again," he asks stopping just down the street from the restaurant.

I start giggling. I meant it when I said too many gin brambles, I was surpassing tipsy right now. Matt raised an eyebrow at me, cool as a cucumber as per usual.

Oh damned him and his damned addiction. Maybe I'm a cute drunk?

"She's a babushka, not a Nana! I say as he pulls my hand back towards him and I twirl into his chest. He lets out an 'oomph' noise and I stare up at his gorgeous green eyes.

"I've had an incredible evening Matt, an incredible day. I know you would probably prefer to be back in Australia right now…" I trail off self-consciously as I say that and Matt uses a finger under my chin to lift my face to his. I know I'm not his first choice, that should be his family.

Heck, I'm probably not even in the top ten. A woman born in the country that killed his father, a woman who is currently being accused of sharing secrets of the country his family have fought for time and time again.

"This has been magical Misha, thank you." I shudder under his touch, and he looks at me, "Are you cold Zótotse?" I shake my head and I hear him whisper under his breath, 'fuck it' as he leans down to kiss me.

Sparks are flying, right? There are fireworks going off behind my eyes. Lips parting I let him explore as I kissed him back with as much passion as I had. Lips being nibbled and sucked he started to kiss down my neck as I whimpered in delight.

"Should I book…" I started to say, my eyes opening slightly to see a man running down the street towards us. Distracting me from my thoughts.

I tried to close my eyes again and focus on the sensation of Matt kissing my neck, kneading my breasts until I opened my eyes and the man who was running down the street was now holding a gun to Matt's head causing Matt to freeze on the spot.

I sober up in record time and can feel my eyes widening in fear.

"Come with me," he says in heavily accented English.

"You too bitch." He says also waving the gun at me in my general direction. Have I mentioned I fucking hate guns?

He whistles loudly and a van screams around the corner and as it comes to a stop the side door slides open and we're roughly thrown inside landing amongst three other men. One of the men holds a gun to my temple as I struggle to sit up.

"A false move and she goes bye-bye," he says to Matt, who looks terrified. How did a passionate kiss end like this?

I mean, just my luck.

Another man grabs a little bottle, pinching Matt's jaw open then uncaps it and gives Matt two sprays in his mouth.

He turns towards me and says "Easy if you just open."

I open my mouth willingly and he spurts a spray of the bitter and gross liquid in my mouth too.

"Do not fight. Much easier if no fight." He shoots a pointed look at Matthew, whose face is marked with worry, and maybe a touch of regret before his eyes grow too heavy and droop closed.

"Motya!" I shout, but my eyes are also getting heavy. "Can you put me against him, please? As a comfort thing?" I bark at the men in Russian, then again in English.

Their eyes opened wide, not expecting the petite lady to speak fluent Russian it would seem and place me against Matt as they cable-tied his hands behind his back. They cable-tied mine too, and I hear the snick of the ties tightening as my eyes close from being too heavy.

Chapter Twenty-Two – Matt

My head is pounding. My shoulders are pulled back into a tight and uncomfortable position because my wrists are cable-tied behind my back. The ties are cutting into my skin painfully, causing a spark of panic to crawl up my throat. I continued my body scan to find my ankles were cuffed with what felt like a short bar between them as well, the metal around my ankles was chaffing, making my skin raw, and painful. I needed to remember my training for both the defence force and the ASIS if I was to have a hope of getting out of this situation.

We were moving, with the muffled sounds of traffic and the smell of petrol permeating the small space. In the trunk, or the back of a truck or something. Making an escape attempt hard, but not impossible. My mouth tasted metallic, and it felt like it was full of cotton. My left cheek was swollen but I could open my eyes. They open to complete darkness which is exceptionally unhelpful.

A groan sounded from my right and I registered that we were moving.

"Misha?" I ask in the dark.

She groaned again and I figured we were both probably in a less-than-ideal state to be in the back of a vehicle moving swiftly down a smooth road. That meant we weren't likely in a rural area which is a good thing, if we manage to get out then we're more likely to be spotted and hopefully helped.

However, I am currently in a foreign country unable to speak fuck all of the language and as a literal foreign spy.

Frankly, I was screwed.

Maybe if they don't figure out who I am, or what I do as a career...

Maybe then I might have a faint hope.

And hope is a dangerous thing.

Because Australia isn't likely to want me back after a fuck up like this, though my brother would probably make it his mission to find me and make anyone involved with our capture pay dearly, hunting them to the ends of the earth until his revenge was complete.

"Matt?" a weak feminine voice croaks out.

"Misha?" I ask back, thankful my voice is starting to feel and sound a bit stronger.

"Where are we? What happened?" Panic starts to rise in her voice and I'm concerned she's also physically hurt.

"Misha, are you hurt? Are you tied up? Did they touch you after I was knocked out? Do you know who might be behind this?"

A barrage of questions might not be useful right now, but if I don't get them off my chest, I'll feel like I'm not doing everything I can to get us out of here. My first step in any escape, is intel gathering.

"I'm tied up but I'm okay. We were drugged with some kind of sleeping spray. I have no idea who might be behind this. They spoke with Russian-accented English, so are likely Russian or at least have lived here since they were children, but that doesn't exactly narrow it down It could be any one of the 144 million Russians in the country. They also knew we spoke English more than any other language."

"We're on a highway, I think. There haven't been any major bumps on the road or major turns that I've felt in the last few minutes. But I've not been awake long. I think we could be in a padded van, or a trunk of a car or something."

As if on cue we slow to a stop and we can hear the gentle click of an indicator flicking on.

Click, click.

   Click, click.

     Click, click.

The van hummed beneath us but I couldn't see any sign of the lights from the back where we were. So our captors had modified this vehicle to stop people from escaping or calling for help at some point.

Professionals.

There were quiet murmurings in Russian coming from the front of the vehicle, "Can you understand them?" I hoarsely whisper to Misha, trying to stay calm.

Best they don't know we're awake.

"They're talking about how happy their boss is going to be when they show up with us. But they're referring to a Sasha and Nikolai.

I suspect they've got the wrong people, but I don't know how we can prove that. They won't trust passports or anything, not these kind of people. I suspect the people they're after probably have the means to change their identities."

The consistent rocking of the vehicle lulled me back to sleep and in my mind, I considered sleep a good thing as I will need all my strength, mental and physical, to get us the hell out of this situation.

A lurch and some shouting in Russian, and a bright, brain-splitting pain hits my eyes as the doors at the back of the van opened with a flourish.

"Welcome to your new home," one of them sneers at me, then barks something in Russian to their counterpart who reaches into the van to grab Misha.

She struggles and starts screaming, which just sets the men off. They laugh maniacally and sneer at her in Russian I'm feeling useless and it's that feeling of complete futility that made me act.

What did I have to lose?

Her.

Getting up to my feet on shaky legs, I took notice of how far apart my ankles are tied, and I launched myself at the man who was currently pulling at Misha's legs to drag her out of the van.

"Get off her you motherfucker," I scream at him, hoping that my training on how to fall effectively and tackling in high school rugby will be handy in the moment.

I take him down, my shoulder slamming into his gut, causing him to start swearing in Russian and then start dry heaving. I land on my stomach and another man drags me out by my arms so only my lower half is in the van, with my head, shoulders and torso bent over the back of the van.

I lift my head at him and roar at the men, "What are you going to do now motherfucker? Fight me like a man, rather than a coward! Coward fights don't count. Untie me and we can find out who can swing better."

He reaches over me, and while I lift my head in an attempt to headbutt him, he grabs the metal link between my ankles and flips me forward out of the van, causing me to land hard on my ass.

He comes down to my face, his breath putrid with rotting teeth in his gums, and whispers "You don't know what we're capable of Nikolai, we will get the information we want. One way," he pauses and looks up for a second as Misha's scream pierces the air, "or another."

He looks down at me sneering, and pulls me up so I'm on my feet.

Before I have a chance to react, he promptly right hooks me in my chin so hard I black out, because of the way my head snaps back from left to right.

I wake tied to a chair, in a completely white room. My legs were attached to the legs of the chair and my chest was tied to the top of the chair, making it impossible to lean forward. The cable ties on my wrists were gone, thank fuck because they hurt. There are thick bandages on my wrists, though they were still tied, but in front of me this time.

All white.   There were no shadows. No other colours. Just white.

There was no sign of Misha. Or anything for that matter.

I was in a sensory deprivation room.

And for good reason. This form of torture, well from what I can remember from my ASIS training, is incredibly effective and has long-lasting mental effects. It doesn't take long for results.

White painted room, completely soundproof, completely smooth walls. White neon lighting, above the prisoner, I guess me in this situation, is used to reduce shadows. White bed and bedding in the corner. Food will be interesting, because traditionally with this kind of setup they only serve unflavoured white rice. Continuing on the white and tasteless thing.

The thought is unappetizing.

I panic slightly, despite knowing that panic is part of why they're doing this.

Sensory deprivation like this is no joke. The human mind is fragile, and once it breaks it can be very difficult to bring it back.

I breathe in for six, hold it for three, and breathe out, and repeat the exercise a few times until I can hear my roaring heartbeat slowing back to normal levels.

I thought this form of torture was outlawed for torture in the 1990s.

I fought against the panic in my gut as a hidden door opened.

"Good. You're awake." An accented feminine voice I don't recognise says.

"And whose company do I have the pleasure of being in?" I ask, my best arse kissing lines coming back to the forefront. It reminds me of a few fucked up times when I was thrown in jail to sober up after a rough night. But that didn't happen in a foreign hostile country.

Surprise registered on her face at my question, "You don't recognise me, Nikolai. Though I suppose it has been quite a few years. Impressive cover I must say. Who is this Matthew Taylor whose face you stole?"

I gulp. Stole someone's face? And knew then we were dealing with people who had some serious cash flow behind them as well as connections to places I didn't want to think about, otherwise, I knew I'd be dead the minute I opened my mouth.

Chapter Twenty-Three Misha

"Alexandra Komarova. It was very clever of you to steal your best friend's passport and make yourself look like her. We've been waiting for a very long time for you to return to Russia. And to bring Niko home? Good work." He purrs at me.

The way he's talking to me, and about Sasha is making my stomach toss and turn more than it was already. They were waiting for Sasha to come back to Russia?

"You've made our job a hell of a lot easier. And what have you learned during your latest stint of time in Australia, pray tell?"

I slowly open my bleary eyes to see a man across from me speaking in Russian. I think his accent is from Southern Russia, but it has been so long since I've had to detect accents that I'm not one hundred percent sure. Also, he's addressing me by my best friend's name which is weird.

The harsh lighting was hurting my eyes, which felt incredibly dry, and the size of the small room was a shock to the system, which is probably why I could also smell the man's overpowering use of cologne or aftershave.

Urgh.

I don't do all that well in small spaces.

Where was I?

Why was I here?

Why were they calling me Alexandra?

Who was Niko?

What has Sasha got to do with this?

Is this why Sasha wasn't keen on coming home?

Did she know something like this might be waiting for her upon her arrival in St Petersburg?

The confused expression must have been apparent, though it surely would have been hard to read any emotions on my face, it felt swollen like I had taken a bad beating while I was out cold. I had read about torture methods over here under the current president's rule, the very same president who was in power when we moved to Australia.

Beatings were the main way to torture people here now, but there were accusations of the likes of poisonings using nerve agents and shootings happening in broad daylight with 'no' witnesses.

I knew Russia was becoming a more dangerous country, but I never suspected that I, as someone born here and having done nothing to aggravate the government or any kind of criminal organisation, would have been safe to visit family at the very least.

I was wrong.

I tried moving very subtly and could feel that I was restrained by my wrists and ankles, even though to someone on the outside of the room it looked like we could be sitting and having a nice dinner across from each other with the table and chairs set up the way it is.

All we needed was the food, wine and no restraints and it might have actually been somewhere close-ish to pleasant. However, there was the issue of the tiny room. I guess for a dinner some may think this 'intimate'. There are better ways of getting to know people outside of a glorified broom closet.

"Sasha, you know what the deal is. You give us the information we want, the information we need, and you'll get to see your Daddy.

We brought you to St Petersburg for this. So we could get you to your family quickly once you've given us the information you've acquired from the New South Wales Parliament." He raises his eyebrow at me, and I'm slowly starting to cotton onto what's happening here, along with realising the cause of some of the random visits Sasha made to me in my office in Sydney.

"Uh, there's nothing new to report on," I say testing the waters, wanting to see what he'd say.

I was trying to figure out if he'd give any further information up, and find out what Sasha might have already divulged.

"Rubbish! I know you planted the drive we gave you in your friend Misha's office." He spits at me.

The realisation hits me then. My best friend did what?
"And while the New South Wales parliament isn't our primary target, your intel may help us get an understanding of what's happening further up the pipeline in the federal government. Did you find any weaknesses or anything more that we could exploit?"

I could feel my eyes widening, fighting against the swelling around my eye sockets, as the pieces of information I'm now getting drip-fed, fall into place in my head.

"We haven't had anything back from the flash drive you planted in her laptop, and I expect Nikolai will have more information as well, he is the mole we have in the federal government at the moment. Having him come here with you, at the same time, has been one hell of a stroke of luck. Heck, it makes my job easier," he finishes chuckling, and my head starts reeling, going 100 miles per hour.

I sit back and try to school my emotions as I take in all the information this man has just disclosed.

So, Sasha somehow planted a flash drive in my office and got someone else to plug it into my work laptop. Was it the one she 'found' when she was helping tidy my office in like my third week? All those months ago? I mean I've not been back since, so I don't know how anyone else could possibly have gained access since then,

I can feel my heart breaking a little at the thought that a friend would take advantage of me in a moment of weakness. I'm suddenly reminded of my Dedushka 'Never trust a Russian with everything to lose, because they will use your corpse as a ladder to get more power'. Babushka used to remind me of his little sayings, explaining how she loved a paranoid man.

I shudder at that, but I know he was right even in death. I need to find out more about why she's been doing this though, what's made her so desperate that she's had to screw over her best friend for a country she doesn't even like all that much, or at least it seemed that way. Did she really love Russia after all?

"Sasha, we don't have all day. If you don't talk, we have ways of making you. I know you have a fondness for Nikolai's new face. We allowed you to kiss before we caught you so you could have a deeper attachment to him, and so we could confirm that attachment." He sneered at me.

Oh goodie, I've been a part of a plan.

"Remind me of the stakes then?" I eye him up and down, trying to take command of the situation again.

"Oh Sasha, if we don't get the access you've been tasked to get, we will start sending parts of your family to you, piece by piece. Nikolai is important, you are not. I have no reason to keep you around except to make him talk, and to appease your father." He eyes me up and down then barks out "Ivanova!"

I gulp at the thought that there's more than one of them. Maybe she won't be as harsh as this man, who seems to be quick to temper and not opposed to threats of literal torture.

"Ah Sasha, we meet again." The woman greets as she walks into the room. She's dressed in a black power suit with a blood-red blouse, and with her pale complexion, bold red lipstick and dark hair, she reminded me of a black widow spider.

Dangerous and deadly.

To be treated exceptionally carefully if you have to handle one, covered head to toe with personal protective equipment and a glass jar. Still, it is best to avoid them at all costs if that's an option. There was a man in the news who 'accidentally' burned down his house to get rid of spiders a few years back, and at the moment I feel inclined to agree with his method.

I gulp loudly as she takes me in, fighting my restraints because all I want to do is back away from her, slowly, and without showing her my back.

"Um, Daniil. Who is this?"

The man looks confused. "This is Alexandra Komarova."

"No that isn't. Have you asked for proof of her mark?"

And this is where they realise their fuck up, right? They've caught the wrong people.

Maybe they'll figure out a way to wipe our memories and ditch us back in Moscow.

I could really do with a do-over. To wipe this day from my memory and go back to the impressive holiday I had planned for Matt and me.

Ivanova goes behind my chair and releases my wrists from their cuffs behind me. "Don't you dare try anything, bitch." She hisses in my ear as she grabs my left wrist to look at my forearm closer. It's then I'm reminded of the half a dozen or so tattoos Sasha has, all in places that can be covered mostly, so I never really see them, but I have seen the one on her forearm.

She has Roman numerals, XXMMM something something. Something to do with how much money her family had on the day the fall of the USSR was made official. She said her family all had it in one way or another on their bodies. A way to remember how little they had before her family and her father, in particular, before they managed to garner massive influence in the country and became billionaires. I always thought it was kind of weird, and a bit controlling but I had been out of Russia for years so maybe it was something the wealthy do over there. Not that I had all that much knowledge of what the rich do over there, or how they act, outside of what I've seen and dealt with Sasha.

I had no such tattoo, they didn't really appeal to me so I haven't thought to get anything permanently inked on my skin. Well, that's quite not true. There have been things I've been tempted to get however I am a bit freaked out about the permanence of it all.

"There's no tattoo, and no sign of attempted removal." She releases my wrist and goes and strikes Daniil around the back of his head.

"Ouch!" he complains grabbing the back of his head.

"What have you told her?" Ivanova snaps at him.

"Nothing," he says smarting still, his pride undoubtably bruised from being hit by a girl.

"Come Danya. We have much to discuss and can't have eyes, or others ears" she says this as she looks at a camera in the corner of the room I hadn't noticed, "watching us." She leaves through a door that has no handle but seems to respond to her being close to it.

She glances back at me and says "You can have your arms if you don't try anything.

We'll be watching."

And the door shuts.

And all I can do is draw my arms up to the table, rest my head against them and cry, cry until I eventually fall asleep.

Chapter Twenty-Four - Matt

There's one thing that having a rough and tumble upbringing in a military community and being the younger brother taught me, and it was how to take a punch.

It feels like yesterday I was going to lessons for karate as a kid so I could be as big and strong as my brother, and technically strong like my Dad.

"Big muscles are all good and well, but you need to know how to use them, Matty".

Then I made sure that Helen wasn't ever bullied at school, threw fists, and received them when boys hit on her or were being nauseatingly inappropriate.

Despite being in a room dedicated to torture, I allowed myself to fall back into a memory of that time.

I caught a boy once hitting on my sister and touching her without permission.

It was my final year of High School and Helen was in her third year, two behind me. You'd think she'd get used to the jeers from the boys in her year group but nope. That and 16-year-olds seem to be completely on a roll this year.

They seemed to jeer and go to considerable effort to make my baby sister feel uncomfortable, she was already uncomfortable with the changes happening to her body and these boys did not help anything.

I was known to pull guys up on their behaviour, so they often made sure they didn't do this kind of thing when I was around.

Helen would never really tell me what was going on when it came to this kind of thing. She wanted to be independent and her middle brother beating the shit out of guys she may or may not like didn't do wonders for her popularity.

That was until she came home crying only a few months into the first term of the year.

"Helen?" I ask, at her bedroom doorway, and knocking tentatively.

Despite being a well-built lad, and a centre for both Aussie Footy and rugby, I have a really soft spot, especially for my younger sibling.

She sniffles but makes a noise of acknowledgement meaning I could come in.

"Who did this to you?" I ask as I scan her, and notice a tear in the collar of her shirt, buttons missing on her school blouse, down to her newly developed chest, and a blossoming bruise in the shape of a handprint on her bicep where the uniformed blouses short sleeves cut off.

I see red. It paints my vision and I can feel my fists clenching at my side and my jaw tightening at the thought of what I was going to do to him, or them when I got my hands on them.

The boys could say whatever the fuck they want to her, but the moment one of them touches her...

Let's just say I hope they like crocodiles.
"Was it a boy?" I ask her.

She keeps sobbing and I go and sit on the bed next to her and wrap one of my arms around her smaller body.

"It was a girl and a guy. He grabbed me hard, and she tore at my shirt, ripping it and causing the buttons to go flying while calling me a slut," Helen says quietly between sniffles and bouts of tears.

"Names Helen," I demand, knowing that I'm pushing her hard right now, but it saves me from just interrogating or terrorising the males in her year group for the names.

"Thomas and Alexi," she says.

I internally cringe. Of course, it was one of the up-and-coming rugby players, and his very popular, very sharp-tonged venomous girlfriend.

I pat Helen's shoulder and wrap her in a big bear hug.

"I won't let them hurt you again. You don't need to fear them, baby sister." I say trying to comfort her.

The very next day I tracked down Thomas and promptly reminded him why he does not fuck with the Taylor family.

His girlfriend decided to publicly embarrass them both by trying to touch up the bruises under his eyes that developed from the broken nose I gave him with her concealer, and he slapped her across the cheek giving her a matching bruise.

Not only did he end up in a very stern talk from the staff, and a suspension from school and rugby, but also given the label of someone who hits girls throughout the whole school. He was dumped unceremoniously by Alexi and was a pariah until the end of the year. Then he convinced his parents that he could be an asset at an all-boys school in Sydney with a solid rugby team. Staying with family until his schooling had finished.

Not someone to be trusted. Not that those in his new school probably ever knew that.

I allow the memories to wash over me.

They might be the only kind of colour I see in this room, the colour of my memories.

Even the rough and tumble upbringing didn't prepare me for the hard open-palm slaps this woman produces every time I give an answer she doesn't agree with.

Or doesn't want to.

Which for the record, is all of my answers.

I know the slaps are aimed at humiliating me, how I, a tough strong military man could possibly flinch when this woman comes into the room and accuses me of stealing my own face.

I mean, who the fuck does that?

I was taught about humiliation slaps during military and ASIS training. It's a tactic that is still used in interrogations around the world.

The sterile room, the uncomfortable position and the beating I obviously received when I was out cold, these days, in these modern times, is considered torture.

I'm not one for violence against women, but in a fair fight, and make no mistake that this feels very much like a life-or-death situation at the moment, I would win.

Also, how could I be humiliated when I'm an innocent man who is currently tied to a chair and continues to have an open palm slap across my cheeks?

I'm not in the wrong.

They cannot strip my pride from me. Only I had the power to give them that. And I've never broken like that for anyone before, I'm not going to start now.

"Nikolai, it'll help if you just talk. I'll stop slapping you if you just tell me what I need to know.

Tell me what you've learned. It'll be less painful in the long term." She pauses for a moment considering something.

"I know we sent you to Sydney many years ago and ordered you to take a new identity.

To change your face," she grips my chin so I'm forced to look at her, "But I never expected you to choose a face that was so opposite to what you were. You look so different now. Where has my sweet nerdy Niko gone?"

She looks deeply into my eyes, hoping to find fragments of the man she used to know. And she might have found it if I actually was this Niko guy.

The desire to headbutt her is strong, but I know that long term that's not going to help me. Even if it would make me feel better to see this bitch bleed for a bit. Okay, maybe getting slapped over and over has got to me a bit.

My shoulders are burning from having my hands tied behind my back for an extended period of time.

I hurt in ways I hadn't felt for a long time.

It's feeling almost as bad as the DTs after I went into rehab and my whole body rebelled against my choice to stop drinking.

Closing my eyes, my mind transports me back to that time, when my entire body was at literal war with my mind.

I know what will fix this. I just need a nip, a couple of fingers of whiskey in a glass and I'll feel so much better.

But I promised my mum and sister that I'd quit. I didn't like the man I was when I was drunk.

A womaniser.

A thief.

A liar.

But this pain is like nothing I've ever experienced. The constant feeling of being far too hot, like I had done a full day of manual labour under the blistering Australian summer sun.

Yet my body was constantly shivering like I was left in an ice bath.

I was thankful I was in a rehabilitation centre for this. I knew I needed the support even though I know my pride would have preferred I shouldered this on my own.

I was also thankful I was doing this while I was still 'young' because there were guys here who were dealing with withdrawal seizures, some who were hallucinating and then there were the screamers.

Grown men detoxing who were crying, and screaming from the pain that they were experiencing. Both the mental side of it and the physical ache in one's body rebelling against the lack of the drug you depended on for so long.

I was brought back into the moment when she goes to raise her hand again, and I flinch against my own will, "Oh pet, I'll be back. Be a good boy and stay, da?"

Shame washes over me, but also confusion. What is happening at the moment? Who is Nikolai? Why is someone called Nikolai involved in this whole thing? Is he someone I might know? What was that flashback about?

I decided the line of questioning wasn't going to get me anywhere so instead I focused on my breathing and did a body scan to take mental note of my injuries.

My wrists were still tied behind my back, tender from the bindings, shoulders screaming from the position. My feet were free, but there was no point in that right now as I was too weak to stand.

My head throbbed, the walls, the table, the chair, everything is white and the light is too damned bright. It hurts my eyes to be open for more than a few seconds.

I don't know how long I've been in here with this woman, but she's brutal and highly effective. I have no doubt she would break weaker men and women. But she's up against a Taylor and we're made of tough stuff.

Fighting the acute need to get up onto my feet and move to curl into a ball over by a wall to get some actual rest I focus on the door the shrew walked out of. It was simple but had a keyhole. And that little keyhole was all the hope I needed. I needed to get to Misha and make sure she was okay and get us both the fuck out of here more than I need my next breath. More than I need rest.

I'd yell and scream for release, but I know other than the room's keyhole, the room is soundproof. This isn't their first rodeo.

But fuck, my blood boils at the idea, and it's at that that I swear to myself that this will absolutely be their last.

Chapter Twenty-Five - Misha

I can hear a scuffle and some yelling from outside the door. And it wakes me from my fitful sleep. I can hear Ivanova screaming at Daniil. "Delat' cherez zhopu Daniil! You couldn't even bother to check they were the right two people? They've just fled Australia, and except for Russia, where the actual fuck would either of them have gone? Which nation would house them knowingly?" she asks him. I can hear his whimpers and it's obvious who controls the situation.

It wasn't Daniil.

I'm all for strong women, but frankly, I still struggle to comprehend how some think that they're best to put down others to climb to power. Surely there's a more collaborative process to becoming more powerful.

"We could just dispose of them?" He says weakly, and my heart takes off at speed with a reaction time that a Formula One driver would be proud of.

Dispose?

I knew what this meant as far as the stereotype went, and I was hoping she would be smarter than that. We both have families who would expect to hear from us. Not that our families are political at all or would expect a ransom for us, but we are just two Australians off the street.

I hear a sudden cracking noise, "Stupid man, why would we do that when we have a literal foreign politician and a soldier fuck up here?" I guess she was irritated by his answer, but I will say that the fact they don't know what Matt does for a living made me feel a lot better. The relief was palpable and exhausted me further.

"I think we.." the voices drift off as they walk away from the room and I'm back to resting my head in my arms, still sniffling and wishing I was back with Babushka. Or back in Bondi with the beach, Konstantin's cooking, my Mama's hugs.

The conversation did leave me feeling a bit weird. I will be the first to admit that I am rather tired of dealing with the hours of questioning and a few hours of being left to my own devices, but I couldn't help a niggling sense of unease in the pit of my gut about the whole situation.

There's a swaying feeling, a weight against my left side and we're travelling backwards, I think.

A constant jerky movement with loud noise seems to completely surround us.

Why are we travelling? My groggy brain wonders.
I'm beyond disoriented.

I groan, my head throbbing with a now familiar feeling of being drugged to sleep and I struggle to open my heavy eyes to try and see what was happening in my surroundings.

Like what the weight on my left side could possibly be.
"Motya?" I rasp. God, those fuckers managed to also affect my vocal cords too. Perhaps, I thought, it was from those hours and hours of crying. Or perhaps when I first woke up and was screaming for help until my throat burned and my voice was nothing but a horse whisper. My eyes hurt from the bright light and feel dry from crying too much and I just want to go home.

I want Babushka to move to Australia to be with her family rather than stay all the way over here. I just want Konstantin's cooking, Mama's hugs and my Dad's comforting words.

I want Australia.

Tears prick at my eyes and slow movements come from my left, I hear a soft sound from there too. I have no idea where we are. Other than no longer in St Petersburg.

I start trying to figure out what kind of transport we might be in. Too bumpy to be a boat or a plane. Perhaps a train or a truck?

The space we're in is pitch black.

"Matt?" I ask in the darkness.

I hear another groan and then "Misha?" comes weakly from him.

Fuck is he hurt too?

I try to go and throw my arms around him, only to discover my wrists are bound in front of me, and by tugging them, with my wrists attached to bindings on my ankles in front of me.

Like I was tossed in this dark space and wasn't going to be found until we reached the destination. Siberia? Are they shipping us off to the expansive tundra to slowly and painfully force us to deal with the repercussions of freezing to death? Fighting for our lives, to hunt, and not succumb to frostbite and hypothermia.

Or are we on an overnight train to another country? To be caught trying to cross borders illegally, prosecuted and never see our families again.

To be housed in a foreign jail to rot. I know Russia's relationship with Belarus would allow that.

Maybe they're sending us to the southern border, where fighting between Russia and former soviet states would make the trip a suicide mission.

I suspect if we made it into the European Union, we could make it back to Australia. That the relationship between the European Union and Australia was good enough to have us simply deported home. Well, at least that's the hope I have. And at least I have hope to cling to.

"Misha?" his voice is tinged with panic now, and I can relate. I'm panicked too. I can feel my heart racing, and the panic sweating is starting.

"Matt. I'm here, I'm tied up and can't really move though. Are you also bound?" I ask in the darkness. I tried to not let my stress tinge my voice, but I wouldn't be surprised if he saw right through that.

I also realise that I've jumped straight to the point. I hope his military sensibilities appreciate my approach.

"I'm tied up to. Any idea where we are? Or how the hell did we get into this position?"

No theories came to mind.

Well, no good thoughts and theories. Everything that my mind is coming up with involves Matt and I rotting in a jail cell until our deaths, freezing to death in the Siberian tundra, or being blown apart by rebels. Who would see us coming from the Russian side of the fighting and could very well fire upon us? We could be considered traitors by Australia if Russian officials report us as missing to claim we were feeding them information. Leaving both of us homeless, seeking political asylum from both sides. Something incredibly difficult.

I was spiralling, I knew that.

I know they talked about getting 'rid' of us and the fear of that also consumed my mind. I start crying again, from the hopelessness of the situation.

The pure terror.

Leaning up next to him I let loose the tears and started sobbing hysterically. The comfort of having him here may only be temporary, I mean, everything at the moment might only be temporary. But it was comfort nonetheless. And from someone who seems to care about me, which while terror floods my mind with adrenaline, warmed my heart a little.

"Misha honey," he says gently. "What's wrong? What's going through that brilliant mind of yours?"

I'm still sobbing, but curl up against his bound body, seeking contact and comfort.

We stayed like this for a while, my sobs filling the space we were in until I cried myself to sleep.

I wake to light filling the little space we're in, there's grates at the top of the wall and now my head throbbing only from crying rather than the side effects of whatever the heck they gave us to sleep.

Matt is sitting up, and I'm leaning against him. He managed to get out of his bindings but chose to stay back with me while I slept rather than choosing to escape. He's against the wall, with me between his legs, head resting against his board, hard chest. I listen for a moment, hearing the constant tha thump, tha thump of his steady heartbeat and his lungs expand and contract with his even breathing.

"Motya?" I ask quietly in the room, and he stirs awake.

"Oh thank goodness, Misha. You're awake. And you're not crying." He pulls me into a hug and I take solace in the way he holds onto me.

"I was worried, you were crying so much. I didn't know how to make it stop." He kisses the top of my head.

"What happened while I was sleeping?" I ask, confused. I seem to no longer be bound either.

He explained that we were on one of the Russian overnight trains and that we woke up in the middle of the night hence the suffocating darkness when my eyes were last open. He managed to get us out of bindings but because he doesn't know Russian he can't tell us where we're going. The door to this cabin is locked from the outside and Matt wasn't able to reach out of the grates to see if there was a note on the door or signage around that might give us a clue to where we were going.

He did say the air smell seems to have changed, going from a forest pine scent to something salty, that perhaps we're heading towards the coast.

That confused me. It'd take a lot longer to head towards the east coast, the trans-Siberian was like 6 days when I was a kid, though we only did it once. Surely we wouldn't be heading down towards Crimea. Or down towards the Caspian Sea. Both, due to instability in the area would be a death sentence.

And not necessarily a quick one depending on who's hands we end up in.

Chapter Twenty-Six - Matt

The train rattled, jolted and groaned as it finally pulled into its final station and completely stopped moving. We had been waiting about half an hour before finally someone, a train guard I suspect, came along and unlocked the room. Probably to check nothing had happened in here during the overnight trip because he looked very shocked to see us in there.

Misha thankfully calmed him down and explained that we had no idea how we got in there and asked him where we were.

"Spasibo," Misha says head bowing in acknowledgement of the fast exchange with the guard in Russian.

Upon leaving us the guard noticed a piece of paper on the floor that must have been posted on the outside of the door.

Misha offered to pay the fare, but the note on the door made him think twice about accepting Misha's money.

"No payment. Just leave. Now. Please." He says, eyes wide and face having visually paled after reading the note.

Okay, not going to argue with that.

We were shuffled out of the carriage and into a brightly lit afternoon.

I notice immediately the salt smell in the air. It brings a sharp sense of homesickness and home even being half a world away.

I also feel vindicated that I was right, we were on the coast somewhere. After hours and hours of countryside air, not even the smell that comes with big cities, it was nice to experience something different. Smell was one of the senses that sharpened massively after I stopped drinking.

I also noticed that all the signs were still in Cyrillic. So, were we still in Russia? Or maybe Belarus? Maybe one of those countries that were previously part of the fallen Soviet State?

I turn to Misha, and ask the important question, "So, where on God's green earth are we?"

"Kaliningrad," she states.

Where was that? I hadn't heard of that city before. Trying to explore a map in my mind and coming up short on that name. Also trying to figure out where we would be on the Russian coastline. Near the Caspian or black seas? We didn't travel long enough to be near the Pacific Ocean.

"Come, I need to find a phone line to call back to Moscow," Misha says breaking my thoughts.

We wandered the streets, looking for a public phone box. Maybe a kind stranger? We had figured out that we had been stripped of our cash and figured that whoever took us might still be on the hunt for us.

I was fairly keen to get the hell out of this country.

We walked into, what I'd deem a seedy hotel, but Misha deemed it perfectly safe and asked to use their phone to call Misha's Babushka back in Moscow. The attendant handed over the phone with no questions and Misha thanked them while dialling a number she had clearly memorised.

Afterwards, I asked her what she said to get the call, and it was that we were mugged at Moscow station as we were boarding the train and that she would be worried about us if we didn't call her and let her know we made it here safely. She also let me know that hotels are one place that typically allows people to make calls when in Russia.

She then said she needed to track down a Sberbank branch and set herself up again with cash, her grandmother had wired some to an account Misha hadn't closed when she moved over to Australia, using it when she comes to visit her homeland.

We left the hotel with directions to the nearest bank and close to a shopping centre in search of money and clothes that didn't scream "I was kidnapped 48 hours ago".

"You're getting your wish of finally getting a hotel room with me Luchik," she says smirking at me.

We were walking near a lake's beach after we found some incredible food and did a touch of shopping, so we had clothes and shoes that don't remind us of the time not so long ago when we were kidnapped off the streets of Moscow.

Misha also bought a 'smart' burner phone and had been messaging her parents and using a maps app to help us find our way around. She pointed to a fancy hotel. I crook a brow at her, wondering if this hotel was a little too upscale. Obviously, she had booked this while we were wandering around the mall or while I was changing or something.

"It's a western chain. And right now, that's what I trust." She shrugs as her way of explaining in the best way she could.

I nod because, damn I got that. I suspect that the last 72 hours or so will take some fairly serious therapy to try and fix.

It feels like PTSD.

We get to the hotel's swanky lobby and wander up to the front desk to enquire about their family and twin rooms.

They had already been booked out, so we booked a night with the biggest bed they had in the hopes I could keep my hands to themselves.

An intrusive thought came into my mind about Misha's handcuffing my hands together and having her wicked way with me, a thought that I dismissed as quickly as it came into my head.

All the same, it caused a flush to creep up my neck and my dick to jerk against the zipper of my jeans at the thought. Something I hoped Misha hadn't picked up on.

We really hadn't had the best of luck finding rooms where there was more than one mattress.

We got up to the room and I flipped onto the bed.

"Want the first shower?" I ask Misha from the incredibly comfortable, plush mattress.

She blushes, "Yes, please."

I somehow find the strength to get up to close the curtains to the room, grab a glass of water, which I promptly gulp down and relax on the bed again, resting my tired eyes and body.

The shower turns off shortly after I have laid down, and there's a prolonged pause before I can hear the door to the bathroom creak open, and I hear Misha's soft footsteps pad quietly across the room to where our shopping was sitting.

I hear a soft whoosh, and my eyes snap open. She had dropped the towel she was using to cover her incredible body. Her long, usually wavy hair was still up in a towel, and I could trace the rivulets of water dripping down her back to her beautifully curved ass, and further down her long legs that seemed to go on for days.

What I would do to have those legs wrapped around me, my head, my waist, I don't mind I just want to feel her. I want to know what it sounds like when she comes. On my cock, on my fingers or on my tongue, again I don't mind. At that thought my dick starts to spring to attention and I groan quietly, closing my eyes.

Why did I always end up with a rock-hard cock around this woman?

At the noise, Misha whips around. "Matt?" she asks, her far too small hands shooting up to cover her breasts and pubic area.

Her hands are too small to cover her ample bosom. She's softly lit by the light from the bathroom and I swear I have never seen a more beautiful creature.

Holy heck. And I'm sharing a bed with her.

Cock, I think down to my groin, I really need you to calm the fuck down right now, I admonish it.

"Ah sorry," I say coughing to cover up another groan of need welling up in my throat. And close my eyes respectfully.

And now I am closing in on painfully horny.

Her slim form covered by her petite hands now an image seared into my mind for all of time.

Fuck.

"No I'm the sorry one, I'll just grab some clothes and change in the bathroom." She quietly mumbles.

Hearing her turn back around and reach to grab some clothes I shoot up from my spot on the bed and go towards the bathroom.

"You paid for the room, you can change here. I didn't mean to make you feel uncomfortable."

I turn to look back at her, clothing pressed against her soft and clean skin.

I can see her face better now that I'm blocking the light and she is beet red with embarrassment, but her pupils are blown with arousal.

She wants this.

I reach down and pull off my shirt, trying to even the playing field with her take a couple of steps towards her, and wait to see what her next move is.

Eyes wide, she reaches up and traces a couple of scars on my chest from a few nights that I have no memories of, then traces the definition of my abs, which I unintentionally tense. I moan and she snatches her hand back faster than I could stifle the noise.

"No Misha, please keep doing that. That was a good moan." I look down at her, pleading with my eyes that she keeps touching me.

She looks down at my cock which was trying to insert himself into the situation.

He's making things awkward.

"We don't have to do anything you don't want to do. Would you be more comfortable on the bed?"

I go to move across the room back to the bed, and she grabs my forearm and spins me into a kiss.

Fuck.

We're doing this.

We're really doing this.

She's kissing me hungrily, a little sloppy but I like it. I let my lips part to let her in and conduct some exploring of my own.

Her tongue slips past the seam of my lips and our tongues tangle for control, deepening the kiss.

All the while her hands are around my back, tracing up to my shoulder blades and back down to my waistband.

My right hand is exploring her hair gently tugging at the wet strands, and my left is trying its luck going down to her breast to play with her nipple. She gasps as I pinch it, and I pull back quickly, "Is this okay?"

She answers by reaching up, grabbing a fistful of my hair, pulling my head back and reaching up to kiss down my now-exposed neck.

She starts to push me backwards and I walk back towards the mattress before falling back into its plush surface.

Chapter Twenty-Seven - Misha

This is the first time I've ever done anything like this, following these instincts in particular. I'm hungry. I'm aching for his touch in places only I've explored and only by myself, and it is making me act out of character.

Usually, I'm relatively shy and demure, but I just pushed a military-trained spy, a 6'3" God of a man onto his back on a king-size bed and I have full intentions of exploring his body and indulging in all these new wants of mine.

Following my need to explore his cock and the hard length of him currently trapped by his boxers and jeans.

I crawl up his body, completely naked. In more than just a physical sense.

Exploring this side of me is also frightening and deeply vulnerable, especially in front of him with the lights on. I'm pushing him back into the mattress while I kiss the scars on his chest. A whisper of a thought, I wonder how he got these scars before he interrupted the thought, and my worship of his skin.

"Misha," he growls. "Are you sure you want this?"

I sigh and look back up at his face, he's checking in with me in the moment. Something I will cherish.

I nod and drop my eyes back down. I get to work undoing the top button of his jeans, taking my time with it to tease him, drawing the fly of his jeans down slowly. This burning desire is making me feral.

I need to see him, feel him, more than I need my next breath.

I'm hoping my actions speak loudly enough for him.

He sits up and pushes me back so I'm sitting on his legs, mine folded underneath me, between his broad thighs.

"Misha. This is a big deal." He says looking me right in my eyes. There's want there. But he's continuing to control himself, checking in with me His blue eyes are blown out so there's only a thin ring of colour with his pupils.

I bite my lower lip and nod timidly; he's reaching into the very tiny piece of me that isn't screaming out for release and desire. At least one of us is in control of the situation.

"I need to be sure you want this. I need your words, Misha. That you want me… All of me. I don't have condoms or protection. And I can go out and grab some but it…" he starts on a tangent and I shut him up with a passionate kiss.

"Fuck me bare then. I need you, Matt. All of you," I say into his mouth, and he moans my name.

"Misha, fuck. I can't be a gentleman. Please. Dear God. I'm clean." He says gently brushing his hand down my torso and reaching down between my legs to start playing with my clit. The gentle rub back and forth over my tight ball of nerves starts to drive me wild.

I release a pent-up sigh as my back bends backwards in response to the pleasure he's stoking within me.

"Fuck it," I hear him muttering to me before his lips and teeth latch onto my oversensitive nipple. I can feel one of his hands down by my damp core, and his other is releasing his long, thick dick from its prison in his briefs.

"Holy shit, you're so wet Misha, is this all for me?" he asks taking further control of the situation.

Fine by me, as long as he can keep up this rhythm he has going on my clit with his fingers.

He can have all of me, everything.
I'm his.

Something I relish, because frankly, I'm just letting my body instincts take control right now, my mind has checked out, and it's in another blissed-out realm.

Can I stay in this kind of headspace forever, please?

I'm not used to letting go like this.

"Matt," I whimper as his fingers slip off my clit and languorously stroked my arousal through the slick seam of me, "Stop teasing me. Please, I need you. I need to come."

"Oh, but darling, I need you to be dripping wet for me. I want to feel your arousal drip down your legs for me. I know that means you'll be needy for my cock but," He says with a sultry tone.

"I'm not little by any means and I don't want you to hurt at all. It can hurt if I'm not careful or if we're not prepared properly." He looked down at me, lust in his eyes, but it was laced with a touch of concern too.

"Zótotse, has anything ever been in this sweet tight cunt?" he asks, fingers tracing around my entrance, and I groan.

"Yes," I say on a breath.

"Fingers?" he asks as he slips one thick digit in gently. It slides in easily because of how turned on I am.

I cry out at the feeling of fullness, but knowing I can take more and shake my head at him.

"Oh, toys then?" he asks before pulling out his finger and flipping us over on the bed, so I'm pinned under his body.

I nod and squirm trying to find friction against my aching clit. Anything at this point. I'm essentially humping his hand, trying to find that sensation that'll give me a heady sweet release. He pulls his hand out from between my legs, and I whimper.

Actually, fucking whimper at the loss of his hand.

He chuckles and I realise, yeah, I need him and his cock filling me desperately.

"Oh Zótotse, so very needy. What do you need?" I respond by grabbing his wrist and pushing it south towards my aching, dripping centre.

He stops my forceful hand brings both of them above my head and holds them there with one hand, by my wrist.

"Last chance Misha," he says looking at me in the eyes. His are blazing with heat, and I just want to succumb to this intense sense of desperation.

"Please, Matt. I've never been fucked, and I need you. I need you to fill me with your cock."

He growls and throws his head back, letting me know he needs it as badly as I do, wrestling for control so he doesn't hurt me.

"I've heard it can pinch a little and hurt for a minute." He says moving his cock back and forward through my drenched centre, coating himself in my desperate need.

"But I will make it good Zótotse, you just need to let me know when I can move okay? I don't want to hurt you; I couldn't stand it if I hurt you."

I nod, and then promptly whimper as he slips inside me.

Holy.

Fuck.

I understand what he means by a slight pinch, but the sensation of him filling me is all-consuming in my blissed-out mind and that far outweighs the small twinge of pain.

He gets himself fully sheathed inside me and pauses. Fucking pauses.

I can feel him tense above me, waiting for my signal, gritting his teeth. Is there such a thing as being too tight? I couldn't hurt him, right?

I allow myself a few seconds to catch my breath and breathe in and out deeply and admire the new sensation of having an incredible man want me so much. And me, the real me, not an illusion of what I could be.

"Please move," I beg. And I hear him exhale in relief.

His hips start moving, slowly at first testing how it feels to be inside me.

"Fuck you're so fucking tight. How did I get so lucky?"

I moan in agreement as I can feel an orgasm slowly starting to build.

"Come for me Zótotse," he whispers in my ear, and I do. I fucking explode and I can feel myself losing control of my body and shuddering and trembling my way through the heady release.

He groans as well, and roars towards the roof as he spills his release inside me and then slowly comes to lay gently on top of me.

"Holy fuck, Misha. I don't think I've ever come so hard."

I nod my head because holy fuck.

I am in a state of ecstasy.

I just feel.

So.

Damned.

Good.

I had never come like that before; toys can't cut it if that's what proper sex feels like.

He slowly pulls himself out. "Stay here, I'll be back in a second."

I lay back as he ran to the bathroom. He comes back only a minute later with a warm washcloth and wipes me clean.

"There we go Zótotse. You didn't even bleed." And I can hear something akin to awe in his voice.

"Are you okay?" He looks at me, concerned. "I didn't hurt you, did I?"

I shake my head. "Luchik, I think I need to sleep." And move to get up.

"I'll order us some room service and have a shower, you need to get into PJs Misha, then we'll eat and snuggle okay?"

I nod and get up to go to the bathroom. Feeling a warm contented feeling coat my body.

Chapter Twenty-Eight - Matt

I wasn't so sure that last night had actually happened, that I had just dreamed up our encounter and how it felt to be with her in that way until I woke up with a sleepy Misha curled up tightly in my arms. Her hair was wildly splayed and tangled above her, with her head using my bicep as a pillow. Her soft breathing against my arm feels like the gentle caresses of a lover, in an almost ticklish way.

Most importantly it wasn't a dream.

It was real.

She's real.

This is going to have real consequences. I gulp at the thought of that. This will have implications for both of our careers. I'd have to leave the ASIS, she would have to weather the coming political storm if that's something she even wants to do. I can fully understand if she wanted to avoid going back into politics right now.

However, what do our careers matter if the people who kidnapped us show up again? Will we always be running?

How the fuck are we going to get out of Russia? Is Kaliningrad even in Russia? It sounds Russian but I really don't know this side of the world well. Or is it another ex-Soviet space? Are we safe here?

Misha wakes then, sleepy and cuddly and my heart rate slows as I watch her come to and stretch her limbs like a cat after a good nap in the sun.

"Morning," she whispers voice still thick with sleep.

"Good morning," I say into her hair, splayed over the pillow like it was, it was hard not to take in the intoxicating smell of strawberries that was present in her leave-in conditioner.

"What's the plan for today?" I ask as I move my hand around to her front and grab at one of her breasts, massaging it lightly.

"Coffee," she moans. "I need coffee before I do anything, and that includes you," she says rolling out of my grasp and getting out of bed.

I glare at her but know she's right. She's probably a bit tender today after our fun last night and I really shouldn't be rushing or pushing her to do things she's not ready to do.

"I'll order some up as room service. What's your usual coffee order?" She asks picking up the handset to the hotel's lobby.

Coffee and eggs on toast arrive fairly promptly and I watch her while she drinks her coffee. She holds the white porcelain cup tenderly, cradling it before gently raising it to her lips. Her eyelashes fan across her upper cheeks as she closes her eyes, and she moans as the first taste, creamy but a little bitter, of her latte, hits her tongue.

"If you keep staring at me, your coffee will go cold." She says to me over the lip of her coffee cup, taking another sip.

Shaking my head at her I take my own sip of coffee, allowing the rich and complex flavours to dance over my tongue before I swallow it down.

After getting suitably caffeinated and sated of hunger, we start to devise a plan on what we're going to do to get the hell out of this country quickly.

"Could we hire a car?" I ask, knowing that this might be an option but also being aware that I am essentially just a sounding board here, having not travelled over this side of the world.

"I mean maybe, but I think we need IDs for that."

"Is there any public transport? A bus? A train? A ferry? Any form of transport that we wouldn't need ID for?"

Her fingers fly across her phone, trying to find something that'll help. After a few minutes of frantic typing, and the occasional muttering under her breath, she speaks up.

"Um, there's a bus. I think if we bribed the driver, we could hide out in the luggage compartment until they stopped in the first major Polish city. Babushka did mention this, and said she can set it up for us. I just wanted to find a suitably legal way of doing this first."

"I mean if that's the best option we have. How many people could realistically be travelling between the two countries? And surely your grandmother wouldn't put you wrong." I was thinking that it's not peak tourism season over this side of the world. But not really being all that comfortable with the idea of bribing an official. What if they turn us in? What if they want more than we can offer them to do this?

We checked out of the hotel and made our way to the bus stop with only the backpacks of clothes and food, everything we had. I know we could have contacted the Australian embassy back in Russia, but I know we both don't feel safe doing so at the moment. Misha made the call through to her Babushka who gave her instructions in very quick Russian on what to do before saying she loves Misha and Misha hung up the call.

We managed to get a lot of cash out and found the driver willing to store us in the luggage compartment to cross the border.

"Misha, are you sure about this?"

She nods saying "Yeah, my Babushka helped set this up. The bus driver is one of her friends from the Soviet Union days. He knows my family. And my Babushka wouldn't set this up for us unless she was sure."

Fuck.

Okay.

Also, low key, what is up with Misha's grandmother and knowing everyone, knowing how to smuggle people out of the country?

This is so risky. Getting caught on the Russian side could lead to a death sentence, and years spent in a Russian jail cell.

On the Polish side, we might be okay, because of Australia's relationship with the European Union. It also means we may never visit Europe again.

We walk down towards the bus station and Misha walks down a nearby street where a heap of buses are parked, all ready to go on whatever journey they are due to make.

The stocky bus driver shows up from behind his bus and nods at us both, motioning for Misha to pay him before then opening up the compartment under the bus that would typically store suitcases, but I guess is for us today.

He looks me up and down before stating, "He will need to curl to fit." And nodding at me to get in. Like this man would fare any better squeezing into a tight space like this.

It was okay getting my legs in, though there isn't much height so there is no way I'll be able to move over the three-hour journey into Poland. I shuffle onto my side, using my new backpack as a pillow before Misha then comes in beside me and does the same, both of us spooning together.

The driver says a few things in Russian to Misha, who nods at him and then he closes the compartment. It's small and musty in here. 10 years ago I would have had a major issue with this but with Misha here it's not as bad. I mean, it's far from perfect but I guess when you're on the run you can't have too many complaints.

"What'd he say?" I asked in the dark, as the engine then fired up towards the front of the bus.

"That he bears no liability if we're hurt, caught or this trip is unsuccessful in any way. We need to cover our heads when passengers give him luggage so we're not seen by the passengers who are doing this trip legally." I nod and grab Misha's waist and drag her into me.

"He also said to be quiet. So no funny business Motya." She says and I can picture her raising her eyebrow, so in return, I cheekily grab at her breast. She swats my hand away with a growl, "Behave." I move my hand down to her waist and pull her into me, "Okay. But once we're back on solid ground, you're mine." And the bus gets moving.

Thankfully there were only a dozen or so people on the trip to Gdańsk, Poland, which meant the luggage compartment wasn't very full and we managed to squeeze behind the various suitcases and tramping packs.

The danger came about 2 hours into the journey when we got to the border checkpoint.

The bus came to a stop and there was shouting outside the vehicle. The compartment opens up and both Misha and I close our eyes and hope like heck that we're hidden enough behind the various pieces of luggage. They took their sweet ass time, speaking to the driver, but leaving the compartment open while catching up. We also heard them get onto the bus and ask everyone a question.

It felt like forever, but they closed the compartment and the bus roared back to life and got moving.

"What'd they ask?" I whisper into Misha's ear.

"If they had heard of anyone trying to illegally cross the border. I don't think we've been picked up by the authorities as such. But we're going to have to fly under the radar to get to an embassy."

Chapter Twenty-Nine - Misha

I found the train to Germany really quickly when we got into Poland, mostly thanks to my phone map app. It was also incredibly helpful that the bus stop was near to the station we needed to depart from. It was pretty much a straight shot through to Berlin.

In Berlin, we'd be safe.

We can get passports and the likes sorted and we can get ourselves home to Sydney. And I mean sure we could do all of that in Warsaw but crossing the border illegally into Poland would be a dark mark against our names here, and getting to Warsaw means getting closer to Russian borders.

While that's not a legitimate threat, it is something I'm unable to get past in a psychological manner. I don't want to be near the country where Matt was tortured, and we were grabbed off the street.

After I told Babushka what happened to us she went into crisis mode, where she became cool calm and collected. Like a switch had been flicked, and it made me wonder what her life was like when she was my age.

At my age, she would have been dealing with Soviet Union atrocities, and the beginning of the Cold War and space race. How'd she handle all of that?

She sent me a ridiculous amount of money and managed to have a friend of hers in Kaliningrad leave us some Polish currency and Euros at the hotel where we were staying. No one ever suspects the Babushkas. And that has me wondering exactly how often my own grandmother has done sneaky things like this before, and if she has a network of people she can trust to help her or her family out in sticky situations.

Matt had contacted his boss back in Australia and managed to get someone called Simon to manipulate the system and grant us access to Poland and the other linked European countries. This allowed us to have visas and report lost passports so we would be able to get to Berlin to get new ones.

We'd both also called ahead to the Berlin Consulate to get our Australian passports rush made, explaining we'd been mugged in Poland. I'm fairly sure this whole thing has caused me to break like five international laws, but all I want is to get home to Australia. We can ignore international laws for a minute, right? Desperate times called for desperate measures.

We jump aboard the train heading to Germany and settle in. The ticket agent had been told we didn't have passports but had the correct visa and we were going across to Germany to obtain new ones.

A few people we've met on the way asked us why we didn't head to Warsaw for a new passport, but honestly, unless it's in a plane heading back to Australia, I want to get as far away from Russia as I can. Warsaw was too close to the Russian border for my liking at the moment. The only time I'm heading east is for Australia.

The train ride through the countryside was comfortable enough. I mean this time we weren't tied up in the dark, and we had the chance to roam about in the train which was a total blessing. It meant when we felt claustrophobic, we could walk down the train and back to feel a bit better about the space. I'm not sure how we're going to handle planes, but that's a challenge for later. Perhaps because we're flying back to Australia it'll be okay.

Because we know where we're going.
We can have hope.

We spent most of the time enjoying the countryside of Poland before dropping into Germany. We snuggled together on a seat and watched the sights go by.

"Thank you for sorting out the consulate and visa stuff," I say to Matt, snuggling further into his side. He's wearing a big hoodie and jeans, which makes him more approachable and less like he's right of the military academy. Cuddly Matt is my favourite, I fully plan on having him 'lose' that hoodie when he gets back to Australia. I get why girls do that now. The size of the one he's wearing would have me swimming in the fabric, and it smells so delectably like, I struggle to put words to it other than to say it smells like him.

He pulls away from me, still staring out the window.

"Did you find out anything when we were kidnapped?"

I totally forgot to tell him everything. I blanked in that second too. How could I possibly have forgotten everything?

I groan knowing that I'll have to rehash some of the stuff that I'm less than keen to bring up in my mind. Things that'll probably take a few months in a mental health specialist's office to sort through properly. If I even can see someone about it, I think some of this kind of thing could be deemed highly sensitive to the Australian Government.

I described that we were in St Peterburg, that they thought I was Sasha, and they mentioned the name Nikolai a few times, so he must be important somehow. I also touch on how they talked about a flash drive in my office, and my reflections that the Nikolai they keep mentioning may have been a Russian mole in the Federal Government.

Something Matt should probably point out to his boss.

They also talk about how they were ready to send pieces of me to my 'family' and how Nikolai was more important than Sasha or I in this case, it was part of their scheme.

Matt described how the spy he was accused of being, Nikolai had a habit of changing faces, possibly through cosmetic surgery, and was nerdy by nature. He also mentioned the conditions he was left in. That bit shocked me. I knew that my birth country's government wasn't the 'good guy' in a world politics sense, but I didn't think that this kind of thing would ever happen.

Actual torture.

I shake my head even thinking about it.

We both seem to take solace in the fact we survived. Even if we weren't sure if we were still being followed, or if they let us go because they realised, they had the wrong people.

"Misha, I've been thinking."

We've still got a few hours before we arrive in Berlin.

I gulp.

I thought this whole relationship might be too good to be true. I mean how can we possibly continue realistically? We come from different worlds; this whole relationship could easily destroy both of our careers if we aren't careful. And Matt tends to err on the side of caution.

"I think I'll file a final report from Berlin."

I look at him then, feeling my eyebrows going into my hairline in confusion.

"You sure? Okay, I guess with that then we'll go our separate ways?" I ask quietly.

I am less than keen on the idea, but the man does have his own life back in Australia and a whole career. A career he's worked so damn hard to obtain. I need to pick up whatever's left of my career I guess and keep on representing the people I was elected to. Or if not, figure out what's next for me.

I don't know if I'd do a second term though. Not after the way the Australian Government has treated me, and how the politics play out in the office. It's still very much a boy's club and I honestly can't deal with a bunch of older white Australian men dictating my work, making me feel uncomfortable, and making my life harder than it really needs to be. I'm not even sure if I want to see out my current term.

"Well, Misha. A lot of my stuff is at your place already," he starts, for some reason looking a little shy, which is highly unusual for him.

"My apartment in the northern suburbs is cold on a good day. And lonely."

We live in Australia buddy, I doubt it's cold on a 35-degree day. But I slowly start to cotton on to what he's asking. I'm surprised, I think. I didn't think this relationship could survive this part of the trip.

"You want to live with me? Like full-time. Like a relationship??" I ask, slightly incredulous, but ever hopeful because I want a repeat of the evening we had in the hotel suite.

Everyday.

Please and thank you.

"Well, I currently live with you Misha," he says with a chuckle. "But yeah, if you'll have me. I'd like to properly move in."

Chapter Thirty - Matt

Our time in Berlin while we waited for our passports and flights back to Sydney was a dream.

I got to court Misha and go to movies and have romantic dinners. I got to show her the little-known romantic side of me. We saw some German theatre and went to a couple of small music gigs in local pubs—nights spent in rooftop cocktail bars, and days exploring things like galleries and interesting parts of Berlin. We always asked locals, admittedly in English, or using my translation app, where the best things to see and do during our time in Berlin might be. And we had an incredible time from asking people who really knew the city.

It was blissful.

Peaceful. It felt normal except for being surrounded by people speaking German.

We were able to find ourselves in those moments and escape the darkness that lingered at the corners of our minds after the kidnapping. We laughed, danced, and just found simple joy in each other's company.

And once we got back to our hotel room I showed her what she'd been missing out on over the past however many years.

I ate like a king, and she, my feast.

I could honestly become addicted to the feeling of her coming around my cock, the pulsating, the trembling, and her insistence that she can't handle any more before I wring another couple of orgasms out of her before finding my own pleasure.

I love the way she looks so sleepy and peaceful afterwards, soft and trusting. How'd I end up in bed with someone like her? How could someone be so trusting in my presence?

It took about three weeks for the passports to process. Three blissful weeks.

One of the nights we took the train across the city and hung out in a bar that played soft piano music while we spoke softly and got to know each other a bit better.

"So why'd you move to Australia?" I asked her, curious. I knew what her file had said, but I was wondering what she thought of the whole thing.

"Dad lost his job," she states while taking a sip of her cocktail. That simple huh?

"That's got to have sucked, what'd you think of Australia when you first got here?"

"You guys talked funny," she says stifling a giggle. I raise an eyebrow, wondering what she might have meant by that.

"It was your accent. I grew up watching the occasional English cartoon and was taught to speak English by a British expat. The Australian accent was weird. Nasally."

Rude.

But probably true.

"It can't be the worst accent out there though."

"I wouldn't say the worst, but I struggle to understand some Scottish, and Jamaican people sometimes."

I laugh, thankful I haven't seen that but at least I know I'm not speaking in the worst accent out there, well according to her.

The next day we visited a few of the beautiful architectural sites around the city and took in the German culture and art. Of course, making sure to indulge in delectable German food and for her, beer at every chance we had, while being mindful that we're not in our early 20s anymore.

Her Babushka made the trip from Moscow to see her, and she broke down and told her everything that happened. Her grandmother had a strange reaction to the news, not really reacting. Misha says she's always been like that, calm in stressful situations, though it screams of some kind of military training to me, though she's of the wrong generation in my mind to have served in any war on behalf of the Russians or Soviet Union.

I might see what Simon can dig out. Because that doesn't quite stack up for me. Not that it's a red flag, but I feel like there is something there that needs more explanation.

I think the kidnapping had worn Misha right down, and she had to relive it when her grandmother visited. Running on adrenaline for long periods can do that for a person. I found out the hard way how fiercely protective I am of Misha, wanting to get up and stomp over to her table at the café where she and her grandmother quickly went over everything, causing her to cry. Anna shot me a glare when my chair scuffed the floor, which would probably have stunned a lesser man, and I sat back down, not needing to see that look twice from her in one evening.

The visit from Anna was short-lived, it was to make sure Misha was okay and able to get back to Australia without further intervention.

The date nights puttered out after that. Misha's energy levels were low, and I was worried she was slipping into a dark place. No one deserves to know the darkness the way some of us have found it in the past. Her slipping into the darkness and embracing it rather than talking to me scares me deeply. I know what that darkness is like. I survived it only because of the faith my own family had in me.

The process of getting back to Australia was fairly straightforward. We couldn't fork out for business class like last time, last-minute flights were cheap, and even with the extra cash from Anna, we were stretched a bit tight in the last few days in Berlin. Instead, we snuggled closely on the plane because we didn't have much choice, but it also allowed me to hold Misha, and whisper into her hair when she was sleeping how much I loved her. Both flights were full, which wasn't ideal. But we managed alright. And the stop over meant I could finally rematch her at her airport people watching game.

There's not much we can't do together.

I was dreading my final report back. I knew I was a bit compromised in the situation, but I was hoping John could trust my professional opinion and understand why I needed to wrench myself off the case.

The visit to Russia did not go as planned. While I was able to watch Mikhaila in her natural and comfortable environment, we both became compromised. We were kidnapped by people unknown which led to us being dumped on a train and shipped across three countries from St Petersburg to Kaliningrad. This also caused us to take some less-than-savoury methods to get out of the country and claim asylum in Berlin, Germany to get new passports. My superiors are aware of this border crossing and the methods undertaken to obtain access to visas prior to visiting the Berlin Embassy.

The kidnapping involved a couple of different elements. One to grab us and drug us with a spray that makes us go to sleep. I'm not sure what the medication was but side effects include sleepiness after being out, a metallic taste in the mouth and a very dry mouth that lasted a few days. After we were grabbed off the streets in Moscow, Mikhaila and I were separated. I was put into a sensory deprivation room, and Mikhaila in an interrogation room. We were both questioned and asked about our involvement in the Australian espionage case. This confirms that there has been a leak in the Australian Federal Parliament currently or in the very recent past. We were called by the names Nikolai and Alexandra/Sasha, which suggests Mikhaila's friend was involved, but also a man called Nikolai was involved at the federal level. This needs to be explored further by Canberra.

I can confirm that Mikhaila was not involved with any espionage but may have been used as a tool or a pawn in this scheme. With that note, I am withdrawing my involvement in this case.

Sincerely,
Agent Matthew S. Taylor.

Chapter Thirty-One – Misha

Walking off the steps from the final plane into the warm Sydney sun flooded my nervous system with pure serotonin.

Even here on the tarmac, I have the strongest urge to run to the closest beach and dig my toes into the sun warmed sand, feel the cold Tasman Sea lap over my ankles and feel the overwhelming sense of home.

Home.

Australia.

But I couldn't do that just yet. There are more things that we need to get done. Matt needed to go to his work to get a few things cleared up, and I had been called back to Robert's office, which as you can imagine I am less than excited about. It had seemed that while the kidnapping had stayed mostly concealed, both of our employers were pretty damn keen to know what the fuck was going on. They aren't alone in that. I too would like to get to the bottom of this, though I suspect I never will know the full story, because of the likes of national security, and because my best friend and person had set my up and then fled. She runs when she is scared.

"What I would do to be able to bury my toes in the warm Bondi sand, with a coffee in hand. Feeling the sun caressing my skin," I sigh out loud hoping he'll take the hint that I'd prefer to head to the beach right now rather than dealing with people who have an inflated sense of self-importance and what is likely to be their persistent and never-ending questions.

He chuckles. He's in a much better mood than me getting off the plane. Probably because he can stretch his legs and take a fresh breath of Australian air, maybe the lingering effects from the kidnapping also wear on him too. I'm not sure he slept at all during that flight. I breathe in deeply, knowing I wasn't going to get a taste of ocean air anytime soon and realise too late that airport air isn't the cleanest but even the air tastes slightly different than it did when we first jumped in a plane in Berlin.

This time we stopped in Doha for a few hours before catching the next flight to Sydney. The layover for this trip was much more subdued with us checking into a pay-by-the-hour sleep place and just being there for each other during the time between flights.

Holding each other.

I know I'm in for hours of uncomfortable conversation with an employer that really doesn't seem to care for me, whether it's because I'm not the "right kind" of Australian, or because I'm a woman I'm not sure.

"Soon enough we will visit the beach, Zótotse," he says pulling me into a hug. We've been much more affectionate since our time in Russia. I think the kidnapping might have bonded us somehow. I'm not complaining. It's beyond my wildest dreams to have this handsome man interested in me.

"Matt, what are we doing? What are we going to do?" I sigh, breathing him in while enjoying the hug, holding back tears.

I don't want to lose him.

I can't lose him.

But I might have to for a time because of our damned jobs, and this whole political thing.

I know I'm overthinking as we cross the tarmac and into the airport terminal.

I mean we did have a chat about him moving in with me, but what if he's changed his mind? I constantly worry that the whole kidnapping thing wouldn't have happened to him if it wasn't for me. That I'm at fault for the torture he endured.

And I just.

I can't.

He sighs, perhaps thinking the same thing. That he doesn't want to lose me.

"I don't know." He whispers into my neck and then kisses the spot he whispered into.

"Could we have a conversation about it once we're back at your place?" He looks down at me with his big beautifully deep green eyes, pleading with me silently.

I nod, and we walk to baggage claim to get our luggage, if only it was easy enough to leave the emotional baggage, we picked up in Russia behind.

The train only took about half an hour to get back to my apartment and we both collapsed on my bed, rather than him going to the spare room.

"What a trip huh?" he asked. I can't figure out if he's been sarcastic or just tired. It'd be funnier if it was a bad trip on some kind of illicit drug. The scarring around my delicate wrists from the short time we were held captive highlights that it wasn't just a horrid nightmare or a bad experience with drugs.

"What's the plan?" I roll over from my back to my side to face Matt. He let his facial hair grow out a little while we were overseas, it has given him a bit of an edge of danger.

I like it.

"I'm not sure what you need to do, but I need to face up at work." He continued to stare at the ceiling.

"And us?" I ask timidly, not really wanting the answer, but I knew it was an important question to ask.

He sighs, "Well that's the question, isn't it? What are we willing to sacrifice for each other? Our careers? Our reputations? Would we need to start over completely?"

I reach for him, putting my hand on his stomach before he moves it off him.

"I think we'll need some space Zótotse. We need to figure out what we want, and then sit down and talk."

He gets up at that, and I think I can hear my heart actively breaking like the tinkering of glass fragments hitting tile.

"I thought you were going to stay here?" I ask after him.

I get no response right away because he is in the spare room, headphones on, and packing his things up. I watched him for a minute, locating every piece of clothing, folding then rolling it before placing it carefully in his large suitcase. Trained at packing up and moving. The precision of the actions and rhythmic motions settled my soul for a short moment before I remembered he was obviously leaving, and taking with him my heart.

Less than 15 minutes later he stops at my bedroom door on the way out of the apartment.

"Misha? Here's your key." He says looking towards me on my bed. Now with used tissues around me, and undoubtedly looking like one hell of a hot mess. He places the key on the tall boy next to the door and turns to walk away.

He stops, his back facing me and says, "I'll contact you, okay? I just want to find out the situation at work. I suggest you do the same. We could look at moving into my place in the northern suburbs, it's bigger than this apartment if things go smoothly. I'm going to leave now while I still can." He then closes the door to the apartment with a soft snick.

Now I'm alone. Truly and utterly alone.

A few hours after Matt left, I tried to reach out to Sasha to see if she wanted to catch up. It would be the typical thing I would do if I wasn't suspecting her of anything, but she wouldn't pick up.

She hadn't sent me any messages either while we had been overseas, and her social media has been eerily quiet. I had a bad gut feeling that she had taken off. Something she does when things get too hard for her.

Misha

> Hey Kostya, I know Sasha comes into Dom with her boss sometimes, have you seen her in the last few weeks?

Kostya

> Nope? Should I have? Are you okay? I haven't seen you in a few months.

Misha

> Yep, fine. I'll explain soon. Maybe next weekend over some extremely good vodka?

Kostya

> Sounds good! I'll book us a table next Saturday here. I'll see you then, at 7.

Well, that answers that. I guess that Sasha hasn't been into Dom since I left for Russia. I wonder if she's been to the university, or work.

I can't really show my face at the Russian embassy at the moment unless I'm being wanted by the government rather than some vigilantes or worse, someone from the Russian Bratva.

I send off a quick email to my old master's supervisor, asking if they've seen Sasha around. He knows we were very close, and I mentioned I haven't seen her, and I'm worried about her, hoping that'll mean he'll release some information that he might not normally.

I can't quite get my head around the idea that Sasha was behind this kind of spying. She's not the person I remember from university. Fun-loving, loyal to a fault. It hurts my heart to think like this but

I know that I've been a pawn in a bigger plan.

Used and then left to fend for myself amongst the fallout.

Chapter Thirty-Two - Matt

Misha

> Matt, I don't know what to do with myself. Peterson told me that any kind of political career for me at this stage would be difficult to get back on track, that there's no point.

I was worried about that. The asshole Peterson, who I have many other choice words for, is old fashioned "Conservative" and has been doing his level best to keep women and people like Misha out of Australian politics.

Matt

> You need to remember why you started on this journey. Why did you want to represent people?

I waited a little bit, but I got no response back from that. I know she's hurting. Hell, I am too.

I found out that her best friend Sasha fled to the United States and hasn't been seen since she got into a blacked-out car outside JFK airport. She's in the wind, Misha has her family to support her, but her friend is gone. The other person, Niko, had been going by Nick Stephenson, had been a personal assistant and media advisor to the deputy prime minister. Nikolai Stephanov, his real name, travelled to South Africa and has disappeared since his landing in Johannesburg.

So all major leads in Australia are in the wind. There wasn't an exodus as such of Eastern Europeans from politics here but this whole thing has very obviously ruffled a few feathers as some other foreign-born elected officials gave up their position in 'solidarity' with the way their Eastern European counterparts had been treated.

Likely story…

I have next to nothing to offer at work anymore, and John's look of disappointment cut deep when I told him I needed to resign. Or at least be considered to be another part of the organisation. I know Misha is innocent in all of this, but the minute I get involved with her publicly, the optics are going to look rough. I don't know what I can do next with my life though. Private security perhaps?

I'm spiralling, and it is taking a lot of my willpower not to reach for a bottle, a coping mechanism I'd used to self-destruct in the past.

My phone vibrates in my pocket, and I ignore it. Wallowing in self-pity, trying to figure out what's next for me felt like my best move at the moment. It stopped and then started again. Fine, who the fuck would want to talk to me anyway?

I answer the call without even looking at the phone resigned to my bad mental state.

"Matt?" Well, I wasn't expecting that voice.

Surprised, I responded, "James?"

"Yeah, listen. I know you weren't expecting a call from me. But I'm back in Oz and I'd love to see ya. I'm based out of the Hunter Valley for the next three weeks and heard through the defence force grapevine what happened to you overseas."

I didn't realise how gossipy the embassy was with the defence force, but it makes sense. I just wish I hadn't been like this. As soon as anything is on the ADF 'grapevine' any kind of privacy can be kissed goodbye.

Bunch of gossiping old ladies.

"Yeah, sure. What about Harrys? Maybe tomorrow?"

"Sure bro. I've got you, and you know that? You can always talk to me, even when I'm being a dumbass and escaping my problems by going on deployment."

I chuckle at that. Because he had obviously been told he does that recently, and it was the truth. Escapism was the coping mechanism all of us Taylor kids had learnt from our parents. It wasn't always the healthiest but it often got the job done.

At least in the short term.

I jump out of my car, a little stiff after a two-hour drive up the coast, but basking in the nostalgia that comes with being back in this part of New South Wales.

James pulls up in a beat-up old Hilux, the kind of vehicle that's kept on base and free for use when people need to get out and about but wasn't anyone's personal property.

"Matt!" I hear him holler at me as he cuts the engine of the old diesel truck and quickly gets out to crash-tackle me into a bear hug. I grunt as I'm hit but lift my arms up to embrace my brother back.

I hadn't seen him since Dad's funeral, fourteen years ago. He's aged, not looking like the man I knew in his late twenties. He's closer to forty now, and surely he wants to slow down soon and maybe stay in the country. Maybe make me an uncle?

"How the hell are you?" he asks as he slaps my shoulder, and we walk into the bar.

We take a seat. He ordered scotch and I ordered iced tea, which earned me some sideways glances from those around us who heard me. James didn't seem worried about it, Mum must have filled him in on my sobriety.

"I've been better man," I start. I explain to him what happened after the funeral, and Mum's reaction to him leaving. His ex-girlfriends struggles before she left the force and moved to New Zealand. Helens sacrifices. My own struggles once most others were healed. At least a little.

He blanched through this part of the story before I came to the latest news.

"And yeah, now I'm here. Misha is back in Sydney I think, and I've been bugger all help to the country in the end."

Saying that out loud hurts more than I'd like to admit and causes James to cringe.

"I wouldn't have put it like that Matt. You investigation, and those early gut feelings probably caused those in Australia to flee as you described. You helped one of our politicians, a group of people who I know you aren't a fan of typically, clear her name. Most importantly you seemed to have found something akin to love. Something that while it doesn't serve the country directly, does serve your family. Remember what Dad told us during that last dinner? Family first, country second. It sounds like you might want to make Misha part of the Taylor family in the long term?"

I gulp. He was always too perceptive and on to it for his own good.

I think.

I do love her.

I think that's what this feeling is.

I actually don't know because I've not felt like this before. And that terrifies me.

"Scary isn't it," he says, reading my damned mind, eyebrow quirked in the same way I've done to Misha countless times.

"I felt like that about Sarah. And look how I royally fucked that up. She fucking fled the country to avoid ever running into me." He lowers his head. I know he regrets his actions. But I know that wasn't the only reason she ran. She needed a fresh start. Also, he fled the country to avoid running into his own demons first.

"Misha has nowhere to run to," I say looking down at my glass. We must look like a couple of sad fucks sitting at a table at a pub both ruefully staring into our drinks.

"Use that advantage Matty. Go fight for her. Who gives a fuck what else you do with your life, as long as she's in it the rest shouldn't matter."

He's right.

Fuck.

He is completely right.

I push out of my chair standing to leave. James grabs my arm, as I turn to go.

"But hey, this time let's not be strangers yeah? You've got my number, and between you and me, I'm sick of running. Don't tell Mum, because I suspect I have a trip to New Zealand I need to take."

I nod, with a small smile gracing the corner of my lips.

About fucking time.

I left the bar, clear-headed for the first time since I got sober, I tended to avoid places where I could crack and a pub felt like the perfect example of tempting fate, and got my CX-5 revved up and going. I turned the stereo off, preferring to instead have the company of my thoughts as I planned on how I could convince Misha I was worth the heartache.

Chapter Thirty-Three - Misha

I started packing up my apartment after Matt texted me. Packing clothes and the like, rolling them like I saw Matt do when he was packing and leaving my home. And to be fair to him, it did reduce the total number of boxes that I needed if I had just folded and shoved them in.

It reminds me of when I first moved in, bright-eyed and hopeful for the future.

I got this apartment a couple of years ago, excited to have my own space. Sasha and my Mama helped me unpack, Kostya made sure once I had a freezer, that it was filled, and Papa made sure I had homemade furniture. Unpacking had been the easy part, and I loved decorating the apartment and filling it with art and items that helped make the space feel uniquely like mine.

I pulled the print of Golden Horn Bay off the wall and could feel my eyes starting to well up. I had worked hard to get to where I am, but this last trip to Russia had set me back.

I pull my books off their shelves and gently place them in piles in study boxes, before placing a layer of tissue paper over them just in case the movers were rough. Putting care into packing the parts of my apartment I know will help me get through the next stage of my life.

Sure, I know why I got into politics, but I am in a precarious situation, and I just want to hide. It's something I've known to do. Run when things get too hard. Flee when things become confronting and scary.

I found a job as a political advisor to an elected official down in Melbourne and they were willing to take me on without references, but I gave them a brief explanation of what happened, and they were understanding about why I was looking to get out and stay out of the public eye. They were just excited to have someone on staff who had gone through the same process as them and knew exactly what being an elected state official could entail.

I was packing one of my final boxes when I heard a hard knock on my door. My family knows what is happening. And they completely understanding about why I'm moving away. Kostya was disappointed, and Papa was quietly pleased, his adventurous spirit probably wanted to join me.

Mama was sad until Papa then explained it's in the same country and it's a reason to go down there and visit. Mama is very much a homebody and isn't a huge fan of travelling or going places when she doesn't have to. She's moved a lot with my father and his adventurous spirit, but she knows what she prefers, and she's made it known to Kostya and me that she'd like us living close by so she doesn't have to deal with even more travel.

The family dinner where I told everyone was met with a frosty reception, perhaps a phone call would have been a better idea. Mama cried, Kostya left the table to clean up the dishes and Papa sat in stunned silence before comforting his wife. I guess they didn't expect me, the timid one, to strike out and try and make my own way in a new city with no support network. The memory of clanking cutlery in my memory was replaced by the creak of my front door opening as I unlocked it and allowed the person outside it in.

The door unlocked and Matt's big frame filled the doorway. He wasn't really who I was expecting to be here. I thought we were looking at going our separate directions after the conversation we had at the airport.

I gave my resignation before he was able to message back, which overjoyed Peterson, and I was pretty keen on just slinking out of Sydney with my tail between my legs. And in doing so before the turmoil of a bi-election starts. I don't want to know the public perception of my resignation, especially with the way the drama that punctured all of Western politics after my election into office.

There have already been marches on both sides, people who speak with an Eastern European accent have been spat at in the streets. There's been outrage from the New Zealand and Russian governments, accusing each other of the other spying on them.

In my own Russian community, I've heard of people considering moving back because they're scared of maltreatment in their adopted home. I could picture the whole situation getting ugly.

I don't want to see the bigotry, the racism. And we can all hope there won't be any but let's not kid ourselves here, this kind of political event can always bring the worst out in people.

There's a look of shock on Matt's face, but he ought to know that I resigned from politics and am moving down the country. He was charged with keeping an eye on me and likely had workmates doing the same thing for him.

His posture was rigid, his facial hair had been shaved off giving him a more boyish look. His body language screamed tense, and it only started when he spotted the boxes. I don't know why he would be surprised. How could I stay in Sydney after everything that happened in Europe?

"You're leaving?" He asks as if it's not obvious. The pile of boxes near the doorway ready for the movers tomorrow probably should have given that away.

"Uh yeah. I need a fresh start. I would have thought your mates at the ASIS might have told you that."

He blushes then, "Well about that..." I shoot him a side eye and glare at him while he continues, "You know how we got visas to get across Poland and into Germany to be there until our passports were remade and we could return to Australia…" He lifts his arm to grab the back of his neck, causing the muscles in his bicep to bunch and flex deliciously as he grimaces, "They were fraudulent. Simon, my colleague hacked into the system and generated them for us. And he was then caught. He'll be out of jail in about 5 months' time."

I'm sure my jaw drops open, but Matt is striding towards me and pulls me into a hug. His friend was jailed for helping us? How could this Simon have even done it? I guess he did have access to all sorts of classified information.

"I've missed you, Misha. I'm sorry I ran, I had things to sort out. I know you also had things to sort out, and I'm sorry I wasn't there for you."

I wasn't expecting him to say anything like this, and my emotions got the better of me and I started sobbing. He was also a runner. Perhaps in future, we should consider running together rather than away from each other.

"Misha, honey, don't cry." He says lifting my chin to look at him and wiping away a stray tear with his thumb. "Whatever it is, we can fix it. We are in this together."

Chapter Thirty-Four - Matt

Only a couple of months had passed since I confronted Misha in her apartment, and now we were moved into a three-bedroom home in Northern Melbourne. I told her I would follow her wherever she was going so there wasn't any point in running from me. And she relented and told me about the job she got in Melbourne.

I had a chat with John who had me removed from active service as an intelligence officer, instead working three days a week up in Canberra as a tutor for those going through the training to be a security agent.

Things are good. Misha started her new job and isn't constantly feeling watched, threatened, or like an outsider like she did in Sydney.

It makes my heart warm to know this.

A feeling I'm told is love.

My ice-cold heart is finally thawing.

My mum is proud of me for taking this chance, Helen was finally in a good space.

I know James is finally settling back into civilian life and has even found love with another workmate who wanted to retire from active service too.

They're happy, which means I finally feel like I can focus on myself and my own love life, Misha.

I know she was missing her favourite food though, so one of the weeks I needed to go up to Canberra to teach I asked Konstantin to come down and teach me how to cook some of her favourite Russian meals.

"Da," Kostya answered the phone to me, I guess despite my wanting to be his brother-in-law he still hasn't got my phone number saved.

"Kon! It's Matt, is there any chance you've got an evening in the next couple of days where you can come down to Canberra to help me out with something? It's nothing nefarious I promise," I start pitching the idea to him in the vaguest way I possibly could.

"Um sure, can I stay for the evening too? Or maybe a couple of nights, I could use the chance to get away from Sydney for a bit." He replies.

We met up at a local café and I brought him back to the accommodation I had on-site for while I was teaching.

"So I want to teach you how to make Pelmeni." Kostya starts as he moves into my very basic kitchen

"I hardly have the skills to boil an egg, are you sure about this?" I ask him, thinking perhaps this might have been a bad idea.

"It will be fine. You've got me for a couple of days and in that time I know I can teach you Pelmeni at the very least. I'm sure you're a good learner and I could teach you harder dishes, but I want to see how you function in a kitchen first before I do anything." He says, starting to riffle through my pantry, obviously looking for ingredients.

"Perhaps the best first step will be to go to a supermarket?" I ask, eyebrow raised. I don't know what he'll find in there, because I've never stocked that part of the kitchen.

"Yes. Let's go then." He says, bringing his head out of the pantry, and looking at me.

It was only a full afternoon before I had the recipe and cooking of the recipe down.

Things I never thought I'd ever be able to give her, love and a half-decent Russian meal were happening. And I haven't been happier. And I think she's happy too.

She's not flinching in big crowds anymore, and while yes, I still keep a close eye on her, she trusts me implicitly.

It's a shame I'm keeping one last secret from her.
Though it's not one I think she would mind me keeping for the short term. Because there is no fucking way I could keep this to myself for much longer.

Things between us are great, and last weekend we visited Sydney for the weekend. Both of us visiting our families. I had her Mum steal her away with my Mum and sister for a ladies' day, and I spoke to her father about getting permission to marry her.

Her brother crash-tackled me into a hug, and the man wasn't small, my ribs ached for days afterwards, and her father's eyes misted up as he nodded.

And now it's the day. She's got a late night as an advisor tonight, preparing for some upcoming legislative updates or something and she expects to be home around seven.

From the front door and down the doorway I have rose petals scattered, and flameless candles flicking giving off an intimate feel leading her to the living room, where I have our dinner table set up with one of her favourite meals, and a glass of vodka tonic for her, water for me.

I'm pacing back and forth, checking my watch and probably treading a hole in the carpet below me.

I hear her car pull up quietly and the key slide into the door.

I dressed up for the occasion.
In a suit and pressed shirt, rather than jeans and t shirt.

I want this to be perfect for her.

I want to be perfect for her.

I hear her softly gasp as she sees the hallway, and she calls out my name. "Matt?"

"Down here, Zótotse," I call back at her.

I love calling her that. My precious, but in her native language.

I can hear her tentatively stepping down the hallway, not wanting to ruin what I'd set up and as she turns the corner into the living room to see the dinner, the real candles and me down on one knee.

Not only do I hear a gasp but the shock has her crying.

Ah fuck.

"Come here darling," I say to her, and she makes her way towards me and stops just in front of where I'm kneeling on the floor.

"Misha, I know we got off to a rocky start. And we wouldn't have ever thought that we would be here, in fact, I suspect the Misha from six months ago might have smacked me in the arm for even suggesting it. But here we are. And it never felt so right. So I'm down here on one knee, asking you, Mikhaila Ivanevna Zaitseva, would you do me the absolute honour of being my wife?"

I know that was a bit of word vomit, but as I say her name I also reach into my breast pocket and pull out a simple diamond ring that cost me a small fortune to present to her.

She nods, her eyes welling up, and I say, "Misha, honey, I need your words."

"Yes Matt, fuck," she sobs, as she comes down to my kneeled height and hugs me. "I would love to make an honest man out of you."

I chuckle, using my free hand to wipe away a couple of tears of my own, I can't handle seeing this girl cry okay? And ask for her left hand so I can slip the ring on her fourth finger.

"You know what this means Zótotse?" I ask her.

She gives me a curious look, and I bend to whisper in her ear, "It means you're all **MINE**."

She shrieks with laughter as I then sweep her off her feet and into the bedroom to make a further claim on my soon-to-be wife.

Knowing we're both in it together and could take on the world if we needed to.

Russian Words and Their Meanings

Zaychik – Little rabbit

Zaitseva – A Russian surname that translates to Hare.

Dedushka - grandfather.

Piter – a shortened version of St Petersburg

Dom – Home

Da - yes

Motya – The Russian diminutive for Matvei (Matthew)

Spasibo- Thank you

Ptichye moloko – A Russian dessert

Zótotse - Precious

Luchik - Sunray

Privet – Hi

Bozhe moi – My god

Durak - a card game played in Russia

Mne zhal'- excuse me

Medvezhonok – little bear (endearment for a cuddly child)

Mat' – mother

Vkhodite Pozhaluysta – Come in, please

Babushka – Grandmother

Vladik – Shortened version of Vladivostok

Delat cherez zhopu- To do something poorly (literal translation is to do something through the ass)

About the author

Aimee (or Amy) is a New Zealander whose dreams of writing something span back over 20 years.

When she's not writing, or editing, she's reading curled up in front of a fireplace, or baking something sweet in her kitchen while listening to an audiobook.

She lives north of Wellington with her partner and wrote this while also working full-time.

Acknowledgements

Holy heck. If you've made it this far thank you! This is my first book, and I am/was terrified at the release it might get. I have a couple of people I want to thank as well.

S. Thank you for always being a supportive partner through this process and only wanting the best for me ❤

Thank you for reading this in one of its final forms and giving feedback so I can put out the best possible 'first-ever' novel! You are the best partner in crime.

My Whānau (family). Mum thank you for wanting to read what I had written (even when it is very much a work in progress), P and A for being your awesome selves, and Dad for encouraging me to give it a shot.

My workmates and Beta readers. Lucy, thank you so much for every hype session around the book and for being one of the first to read my draft. I hope the product lives up to your dreams. Also, I'm sorry for teasing you with spoilers.

I couldn't have done this without you, Krysdelle, an incredible human and fantastic beta reader. Yes, add editor to your LinkedIn/CV. In fact, please do. I will back you up for it.

Thank you both for your support, input and excitement around all of this. And for accepting the challenge of Beta reading for me. I legit could not have done this without you both. And I mean that. I could not have done it without either of you ❤

SC, yeah boi, you've got a shout-out. Also note, that I didn't kill off the character named after you, I just jailed him...

My team! The best hype team out there. Thank you to every single one of you in P&M for the hype and excitement about me doing this in my 'spare' time. I owe you guys more cookies than I can bake.

My bookstagram besties, for your patience and hype around this book. I am so thankful for every one of y'all who reached out and had a conversation with me about this. I hope it lives up to your expectations!!

And to you, dearest reader. From the bottom of my heart, thank you. This book was written with the mindset that at some point someone will read it, and you have. And the idea that anyone who wants to read something I've written still to this day blows me away (should probably bring that up to my therapist).

You can find me at @AimeeBlancAuthor on Instagram or you can email me at aimeeblancauthor@gmail.com.

Want the epilogue? Sign up for my newsletter from my website to find out what's next for Misha and Matt, and to be the first to hear more about the next story from me.

Who doesn't love an exclusive?